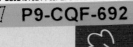

ballistic
BUGS

the misadventures of WilliE PlummeT

PAUL BUCHANAN
& ROD RANDALL

CP

SAINT

JF
RAN

The Misadventures of Willie Plummet

6006

Cover illustration by John Ward.
Back cover photo by Ira Lippke.
Cover and interior design by Karol Bergdolt.

Scripture quotations taken from the HOLY BIBLE, NEW INTERNATIONAL VERSION®. NIV®. Copyright © 1973, 1978, 1984 by International Bible Society. Used by permission of Zondervan Publishing House. All rights reserved.

Copyright © 1998 Rod Randall
Published by Concordia Publishing House
3558 S. Jefferson Avenue, St. Louis, MO 63118-3968
Manufactured in the United States of America

Library of Congress Cataloging-in-Publication Data

Buchanan, Paul, 1959-
    Ballistic Bugs / Paul Buchanan and Rod Randall.
    p.   cm. — (The misadventures of Willie Plummet)
    Summary: Hoping to win the cash prize in the Glenfield Bug-Off, seventh-grader Willie Plummet invents a concoction to attract the world's largest locust and then must examine his Christian values as he tries to deal with the consequences.
    ISBN 0-570-05044-8
    [1. Contests—Fiction. 2. Inventors—Fiction. 3. Christian life—Fiction.] I. Randall, Rod, 1962- . II. Title. III. Series: Buchanan, Paul   Misadventures of Willie Plummet.
PZ7.B87717Bal 1998
[Fic]—dc21
                                       97-34970
                                         AC

2   3   4   5   6   7   8   9   10   07   06   05   04   03   02   01   00   99   98

For my children,
Taryn, Lauryn, and Corbin Randall

Contents

The Big Bug-Off

The giant locust buzzed through the air just above my head. I ducked low, fearing it would grab my hair and take me with it. The thing was big, brown, and ugly.

Talk about the kind of bug dreams are made of! This baby was guaranteed to win me, Willie Plummet, first prize in the Glenfield Bug-Off. I wanted to win in a bad way. I'm talking $5,000 bad. That's how much first prize paid. But to collect the cash, I'd have to catch a locust as big as the one dive-bombing my head. It sounded like a bumblebee on steroids and looked meaner.

Gripping my net, I jumped and swung. *Whiff.* Strike one. The locust buzzed off, laughing. I'm not sure about the laughing part, but the buzzing definitely had a higher, perkier pitch when I tripped and hit the ground.

"Smooth move, locust lips," my brother, Orville, chided. He sat in a lawn chair in the sun, rubbing SPF-40 sunscreen on his freckled shoulders. My big brother has the same red hair, and probably the same number of freckles, that I have.

I picked myself up and scrambled after the gloating locust. *Never surrender,* I told myself. *You're bigger than the locust—at least a little. Don't let a spiny-legged, small-brained bug get the best of you.*

The locust must have sensed my superiority because it retreated to a maple tree in our front yard. A branch dipped under the locust's weight, bringing it just low enough to reach. All I had to do was climb on the hood of Orville's pickup.

I glanced at Orville to make sure he wasn't looking. He had closed his eyes and leaned back to soak up the rays. I placed my foot on the front bumper to climb aboard.

"Don't even think about it!" Orville warned.

When I looked back, his eyes were still closed. How had he seen me? He's worse than Mom.

"Orville, be quiet," I whispered in his direction. "You'll scare it away." The locust fluttered its wings as if to fly, then drew them back inside its shell.

"I'm serious, Willie," Orville continued. "Get off my truck before I crush you like a strawberry."

"Don't worry," I said. "I'll take off my shoes." I let them drop to the ground.

"If anything happens to my truck, you're ..."

"Nothing's gonna happen," I promised. Edging forward, I stepped onto the hood.

Bad idea for two reasons. One, the hood was skillet hot. And two, my socks had holes in them.

"Yeowww!" I wailed, trying not to spook the locust. It let out a faint chirp, which I'm sure was a chuckle, but it didn't fly away.

Teetering on my heels, I avoided standing on one piece of skin for too long. I had to move quickly. I raised my net to within a few feet of the locust, then slowly closed in. Careful. Get ready to pounce. Now!

I brought the net down—too fast. I lost my balance. The locust sprang into the air, its wings in overdrive. Wobbling off-balance, I stepped backward. I landed on the hottest section of the hood yet. My foot felt like a piece of fried bacon. Spinning around, I lost my balance again. Instinctively, I used my knee to break my fall. Not a smart move.

Bam! The hood dented like aluminum foil. I rolled off the truck and looked back. A little dent, the size of Jupiter, creased the precious metal.

"If that looks as bad as it sounded ..." Orville cried. He jumped up and marched toward his truck.

Rather than wait for my brother's response to the planet-size dent, I did what any quick-thinking 13-year-old little brother would do.

I ran.

"Willie!" Orville shouted.

The chase was on and the stakes were high. If Orville caught me, I'd have too many broken bones to catch a prize-winning locust. Don't get me wrong. Orville is a great older brother. Because he is 16, he can drive me around. Because he is mostly muscle, he can defend me. In fact, he rarely lets anyone pick on me. He feels that's his job. And believe me, he doesn't need any help.

I headed for the sliding door. Orville closed in—I wasn't going to make it. I reached for a patio chair and swung it behind me. It landed right in front of Orville. He attempted to hurdle it but tripped over the chair and smashed to the ground. As I passed through the glass door, I wanted to ask, "Have a nice trip?" but I thought that might be pushing it. The Lord had been kind enough to me already.

After locking the door, I lunged across the family room, still watching over my shoulder. Big mistake. Amanda, my 18-year-old sister, was hemming a dress, and I ran into her. We both tumbled to the carpet.

As I got to my feet, Amanda let out a bloody scream, a lot like Orville's —with the exception of her girlish pitch. Looking back, I knew why. Her coffee had spilled all over the dress she was sewing for the Beauty Bug Pageant. The steam lifting from the fabric was nothing compared to the smoke pouring from her ears.

Good thing I had a lock on my bedroom door. If only I could make it there alive. Sprinting for the stairs, I heard the back door open.

"Stop him," Orville yelled as he thundered across the kitchen.

Amanda closed in from the family room. Maybe they would bump into each other at the bottom of the stairs, fall down, and start yelling at each other. I'd get off scot-free and even pause at the top of the stairs to watch them fight. Yeah right. In my wildest Willie dreams.

By the time I made it halfway up the stairs, Orville and Amanda arrived at the bottom. Instead of colliding, they turned on a dime and ran shoulder to shoulder. They resembled a military death squad, united once again for a common mission: to destroy their innocent little brother, whom they secretly admired.

"Stop now and you *may* live," Orville called out.

"Never," I replied, taking the stairs three at a time. Too bad Orville and Amanda took them four at a time. They closed the gap.

I reached the top of the stairs and ran for my room. The door was open. If I could just make it inside and turn the lock, I'd use my bed as a barricade.

Orville and Amanda topped the stairs. Orville pulled ahead of her. His breath puffed behind me. I lunged ahead, desperate to escape.

A Wave Ruler XT for Me

Jumping into my room, I slammed the door and locked it in one swift movement. Orville and Amanda pounded on the door, nearly knocking it in, which is what they wanted to do with my teeth.

I didn't answer their yells, knowing that no matter what I said, it would only make things worse. After several minutes of telling me what I was in for later, they gave up. We had been through this type of thing before. Orville and Amanda knew that until Mom and Dad came home, there was no way I was coming out.

Plopping down on my bed, I felt guilty and depressed. I had messed up Orville's truck and I could never catch a prize-winning locust while I was cooped up in my room.

For five years I had looked forward to this week. That's how often the giant locusts returned to Glenfield. Once every five years they came by the thousands, hundreds of thousands, even.

For years it was just a big nuisance. Then someone got the idea that we should make the best of it.
After a lot of planning, the Glenfield Locust Festival
was born.

For one week in July the whole town goes gaa-
gaa with locust activities and events. There's a Locust
Luau, a Beauty Bug Pageant, and best of all, the Bug-
Off. Like most towns, Glenfield has a chili cook-off
every summer during the fair. But unlike any other
town, we also have a Bug-Off. It has nothing to do
with food. It has nothing to do with "get lost," which
is normally what the phrase "bug off" means.

The Glenfield Bug-Off is all about catching the
largest locust. To qualify, the locust must be alive.
Whoever wins becomes the Locust Legend for the
next five years. The winner also gets a check for
$5,000, plus his or her picture in the paper, not to
mention the admiration of the entire town.

Marvin Bink was the runaway favorite to win.
He'd won the Bug-Off five years ago. I still remember
Marvin's acceptance speech and watching him at the
podium, holding that oversize, three-foot wide check.
Since then I had spent days, weeks, months, even
years, dreaming about what I would buy with the
money—a Wave Ruler XT. It was just like a Jet Ski,
only cooler—way cooler.

Too bad for me that while the first locusts arrived
in town, I was locked in my room until my mom and
dad came home from shopping. Looking out my win-

dow, it was almost too painful to watch. Locusts filled the afternoon sky like gold coins from heaven. Some even hovered in front of my window as if to say, "Having fun in there, Willie? We sure are." That hurt.

I knew I should have closed my window shades, or at least closed my eyes. But I couldn't. I was overcome with locust fever. I just stared, longingly.

Then I spotted him. My bad day got worse. *Lord, why me?* Not him, anyone but him! Marvin Bink strutted down the sidewalk. Children circled him, chirping one compliment after another. He soaked in their praise, then waved them off. Looking from side to side, as if to make sure no one was watching, he walked between two houses, then crossed a field toward Shadow Grove.

"So *that's* it," I said out loud. Maybe getting trapped up here isn't such a bad thing after all. Now I know where to look for the big fat locusts. Shadow Grove.

I heard my parents drive up. Perfect timing. I'd patch things up with Orville and Amanda, have a little dinner, then grab a flashlight and resume the hunt.

Before dinner I gave Samantha a quick call. She was one of my best friends. Sam wouldn't pass on an adventure for anything, which made her even more cool to hang out with. But this time she surprised me.

"I'm too tired," Sam complained.

"What are you, a girl?" I chided.

"Actually, I am a ..."

"This is summer," I cut in. "You can sleep any-time—all the time. It's not like you have a job or any-thing."

"I do now," she explained.

"Since when?"

"Since my Aunt Kathy's bee farm ran into trou-ble."

"What kind of trouble?" I asked.

"Locust trouble," Sam told me. "They're 10 times bigger than the honeybees and twice as mean."

"But the bees have stingers," I argued.

"So what? The locusts' shells are like steel. You know that."

Sam was right. The locusts had shells that would make a turtle jealous.

"The bees are leaving the hives in droves," Sam continued. "The ones that aren't leaving are turning out bad honey."

"Bad Honey?" I chuckled. "Sounds like an '80s rock band. I think my dad has a record by them."

"That's not funny, Willie," Sam told me. "My aunt's in trouble. The farm is a disaster."

"You should have heard the record."

After a long pause, with zero laughter coming from Sam's end of the phone, she continued. "My Aunt Kathy lives all alone," Sam said. "She needs our help. What do you say? Will you help me tomorrow?"

"No way. There's a $5,000 Bug-Off to win. Why would I want to risk getting stung by a bunch of bees?"

"Come on, Willie."

"Forget it. What part of *no* don't you understand?"

"What part of the Bible don't *you* understand? Obviously not *'Love your neighbor as yourself.'* "

Ouch. That hurt. I started to feel like maybe I should help. Sam had never let me down. But winning the Bug-Off meant too much to me. I decided to try a different approach. "If I help, how much money will I make?"

"Willie!"

"I'm serious. You should see the crater-size dent I put in Orville's truck. I need some serious cash—fast!"

"Just use your savings to fix the truck. You have enough."

"I know. But my savings, along with the Bug-Off prize money, is just enough to buy the Wave Ruler XT."

Sam exhaled. "My aunt's bills are piling up fast, but I'm sure she'll pay you what she can."

"In other words, not much," I replied. "Sorry, Sam, but I've spent too long dreaming about the Wave Ruler XT. I can't lose a day helping your aunt."

"Willie, your attitude is …"

"Gotta go, Sam. Later." I hung up before she could pour on more guilt. Then I bounced downstairs, ready to fill my belly with a mountain of food.

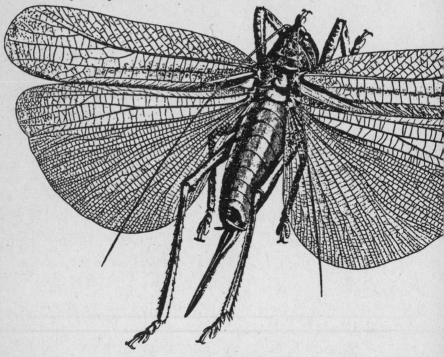

The Mother of All Locusts

So much for *a mountain of food*. My parents brought home sushi for dinner. Ixnay on filling my belly. At least that was my opinion. My mom seemed to think otherwise. She scooped out jumbo helpings for each of us kids. The fish on my plate smelled like the garbage disposal.

"Mom, I can't eat this," Amanda stated. "What if I have an allergic reaction and vomit? The Beauty Bug Pageant is only five days away."

"Is barfing grounds for disqualification?" I asked, looking at Orville.

"Only if it's on the judges," Orville explained. "But just to be safe, I'll have her's."

"Her barf?" I asked.

"No. Her sushi, you twerp." With a swipe of his fork, Orville cleaned Amanda's plate and swallowed it down. Normally Orville avoided gross food, especially Dad's chili. But when it came to take-out, he couldn't get enough. Whatever Mom brought home, pizza, tacos, hamburgers—even sushi—he devoured.

I slid my helping onto Orville's plate. "Have some more, Orville. It's brain food." I wanted to add, "You can use it," but after the incident with his truck, I figured I'd better keep my mouth shut.

Dad chewed a piece of something rubbery and white, then turned his attention to me. "Willie, the dent you put in your brother's truck will be expensive to fix."

"Don't worry, Dad. The Bug-Off prize money is practically mine," I assured him.

Dad frowned. "I'm afraid you can't depend on that, Willie. You'll need a more reliable source of income." I didn't like the way that sounded. It had *child labor* written all over it.

"Just give me your savings," Orville put in. "Then we'll call it even."

"Forget you," I said. "That's Wave Ruler XT money."

"Perhaps I may have a solution," Dad continued. "Just today I was noticing how much work needs to be done at Plummet's Hobbies. For starters, all my model planes need dusting." A soft glaze filled my dad's eyes as he visualized each one. "Then there's the new glue that needs pricing. I'd also like you to check the lids of all the glue bottles to make sure they're tightened properly. I know I've said this before, but it's worth repeating, if the lid isn't tightened just so, there's a chance the glue's adhesive properties will be reduced."

I'd heard enough. Bring on the bees. They could use my body for a dartboard. I'd even help them keep score. Anything but spend a day at Plummet's Hobbies tightening glue caps. Maybe I could even catch one of those giant locusts that scared off Aunt Kathy's bees. It made sense. Why would the locust command send in anything less than the best troops to wipe out a hive of bees? This was perfect—not only would I catch some giant locusts and make a pile of money, but the bees would be indebted to me for life.

"Don't even think of stinging Willie Plummet," they would buzz to one another. "He's the man."

"Sorry, Dad," I said when he paused to take a breath. "I'm going to work for Sam's aunt. Her bees are turning out bad honey."

"Bad Honey? I have a record by them. Let's put it on," Dad said with enthusiasm.

"Not right now, dear," Mom said. "We're trying to enjoy our meal."

"Honey?" Orville said. "Now you're talking." He went to the cupboard and brought back a jar of honey. We watched in awe as he poured it all over his sushi.

Amanda covered her mouth. "You're not really going to ..."

Orville cut her off by shoving an entire raw squid, dripping with honey, into his mouth. I had to look away.

Dad patted Orville's back. "Sam's aunt would be impressed, son."

"So would Ripley's Believe It or Not," Amanda added, excusing herself from the table. "Bradford is scheduled to call me at seven, and I need to get ready."

She wasn't joking. Amanda spends more time preparing for a phone call than most girls do for dates. Mouthwash, makeup, lipstick—she goes through the whole routine. She even drenches herself in expensive perfume. The phone smells like her for days afterward and rubs off on unsuspecting little brothers.

One time I made a call right after Amanda, then went out and bumped into Leonard "Crusher" Grubb. "Nice perfume, pretty boy," Crusher teased. "Where's your dress to go with it?" With Crusher's friend's gathering around, I was lucky to make it home alive.

"So when do you start your new job?" Mom asked, bringing me back to the present.

"Tomorrow. I should be there most of the day."

Orville grabbed my collar, his fish breath blurring my vision. "You mean most of the *week*. That's how long I'm giving you to come up with the cash."

"How about if I bring you some bad honey to make up the difference?" I suggested. But Orville just shook his head and tightened his grip.

I choked out a promise to pay Orville in full. He released me, and I dashed to get to the phone before Amanda reached it in all her smelly glory. I punched in Felix's number. After a ton of persuading, Felix promised to meet me at Shadow Grove. Like Sam, he was one of my best friends. Unlike Sam, Felix disliked adventure—especially if it meant hunting giant locusts in the woods at night.

"What if we get stung?" he asked over the phone.

"Locusts don't sting," I told him.

But when Felix finally showed up, he looked more protected than an armored car. He had on hiking boots, welding mitts, a bike helmet, ski goggles, and a vinyl rain suit. The vinyl squeaked like a squeegee on glass every time he moved.

"Felix, you're such a spazz," I laughed. "I told you locusts don't sting."

"True. But after a little research, I learned that though they may not sting, they *do* bite. And the bigger they are, the more it hurts."

"Whatever you say," I said, trying not to lose my patience. "Now come on. Do you want to win or not?"

"Or not."

"Fine. When we capture a world-record locust, I'll take the credit and keep the money just to make you feel better." I grabbed a flashlight and my insect collector kit and we set off for Shadow Grove.

Shining my flashlight through the trees, I remembered why it was called Shadow Grove. Tree branches arched above their trunks, covering the ground with shadows. *Dark* shadows.

"You're sure Marvin Bink is in there?" Felix asked, refusing to go any farther.

I put my arm on Felix's shoulder. "The last time I saw Marvin, he was headed this way. But so what if he isn't here? All we care about is the money. Five thousand dollars split between me and you, 70–30, even-steven."

"What?" Felix choked. "Since when is 70 percent for you and 30 percent for me even?"

"Let's not split hairs, ol' buddy. You wouldn't even be out here if it weren't for me."

"That's for sure," Felix grumbled. Heading off again, we stepped carefully through Shadow Grove. Not a star could be seen through the thick leaves overhead. The leafy canopy looked more like the ceiling of a cave than tree branches. I breathed in the stuffy air. Studying the ground, Marvin's footprints were nowhere in sight.

After taking a few more steps, we no longer worried about Marvin. Locusts by the thousands buzzed in and out of our flashlight beams. They clung to tree trunks and covered the ground like carpet.

"Eureka!" I shouted. Removing my net from my insect collector's kit, I took a swipe and caught a locust. But after a closer look, I let it go. It was no bigger than a beetle.

"Wait a second," Felix said, squeaking up beside me like a penguin. "They're *all* tiny." I studied the cloud of insects buzzing around me. Felix was right.

"What a waste," I grumbled.

"Shadow Grove must be a nursery for locusts," Felix said. Moving deeper into the woods, we hoped some big ones would appear, but they never did. Jumping around, I tried to dodge the locust babies. But there were too many. I landed right on one. *Crunch!* Then another. *Crunch!* I jumped back and forth like a football player going through tires. *Munch-crunch. Crunch-munch.* That went on until I felt a dampness soaking through my socks.

"Oh no," I whined, remembering the holes in my old tennis shoes. Sitting down, I checked the damage. Sure enough, my socks were full of locust guts. Brown and yellow ooze dripped from the white cotton.

"Great," I muttered. I removed my socks and tossed them into a bush. Even after the socks landed, the bush continued to rustle. I shined my light at the branches, waiting for a raccoon to come crawling out.

"Felix, get over here," I commanded, carefully standing on my bare feet. With all the spiny locusts on the ground, I wasn't about to move. Puffing hard,

Felix waddled over. Sweat dripped down his chin from the heat of his thermal protective suit.

"What's under the vinyl?" I asked, staring at his massive rain suit.

"Two pairs of long underwear, sweats, and denim overalls, all wrapped with a hundred yards of ace bandage."

"Are you okay?" I asked.

"Yeah, fine," he said with a gasp.

"Good, 'cause I need a piggyback ride over to that bush."

"Just put your shoes back on."

"No way. They're filled with locust guts." I jumped on Felix's back before he could object. With his flashlight guiding our way—and mine focused on the bush—he stumbled forward.

As we neared, the bush rustled again. I focused on the leaves, trying to see through them. Felix shook all over, either from fear of the thing in the bushes or from my weight.

"Careful, big fella," I cautioned Felix, patting him on the shoulder. I looked down and swallowed hard. There were enough spiny locusts beneath us to turn my feet into grated cheese. Stepping from side to side, Felix tried to keep his balance and hold me at the same time, but he couldn't. His foot tripped on an exposed root. We tumbled to the ground, landing at the base of the bush.

I stared in horror as the shaking spread from the center of the bush and swept over every branch, like a grizzly bear rudely awakened from hibernation. I tried to scramble backward but my hand landed on a locust's spiny shell.

"Ouch," I wailed, shaking it loose.

Felix stayed on his back, his eyes shut, mumbling a multitude of prayers. More and more locusts began to gather, buzzing in a frenzy. The leaves split apart. A locust's head, bigger than my head, appeared from the bush. It towered over me. Its sinister eyes burned with hate. I couldn't scream. I couldn't move. I just stared, petrified. The mother of all locusts stared me down. I tried to reason with her.

"You mean those were *your* babies? I *tried* to dodge them."

The locust shrieked out a piercing hiss. My eardrums nearly burst. So much for reason. I scrambled backward in terror. Rising to my feet, I turned to run. I could hear the monster behind me, snapping twigs, hissing with rage.

I ran a few yards, then tumbled to the ground. A sharp burning sensation shot through my foot. "Yeow," I screamed, removing the locust shell from my skin. I clutched my foot. Blood oozed past my fingers.

"Felix, run!" I yelled, picking myself up, determined to hop on one foot if necessary.

I listened for the giant locust, anticipating the hiss of doom. My doom. I could see the headline now: "Willie Plummet Crunched by the Mother of All Locusts."

Teetering back and forth, I balanced on one foot. I held my flashlight like a club, ready to fight back before the giant locust's pincers cracked my skull like an egg. I waited for the gruesome buzz of death—I turned around, ready to start swinging. What I saw left me frozen in shock. A half-human, half-locust creature stepped into full view.

I stared in awe, thinking it would sprint forward and latch onto my neck with its fangs. Or maybe it would take flight and take me with it. I expected it to do anything but laugh.

That's right, the human locust laughed! If I hadn't been frozen in terror, I would have gone over and punched it in the chops. Instead, I wobbled off balance and fell down again. The bug stepped over Felix and strutted toward me, laughing with each step until it was only a few feet away. Then the mother of all locusts reached up with its human hands and popped off its own head.

Marvin Bink stared down at me with a smug look on his face. "Willie, even *you* know better than to hunt locusts in bare feet. Would you like me to call your mommy?"

"Real funny," I grumbled, working my way back to my shoes. They may have been full of locust guts, but at least they'd get me home.

"So this is the secret," I said, taking hold of Marvin's mask. Even up close it looked just like a locust's head. It had glossy black eyes, a triangle-shaped mouth, bony lips, and two antennae.

"Secret?" Marvin asked, trying to look surprised. "What do you mean?"

Felix wobbled over. "For winning. With this on your head, the locusts won't fly away. Catching them would be a cinch."

Marvin grabbed his mask. "I'm not using this to win. I just wear it to impress the little kids ... like you."

"Sure," I said, rolling my eyes. "Whatever you say."

"There's no gimmick, Willie," Marvin insisted. "Winning comes down to long hours and hard work."

I couldn't believe what he'd said. The most dreaded of all nouns: work. No kid willingly did anything that resembled work, let alone *hard* work. Marvin had said too much. His secret was obvious. And if it worked for him, it would work for me too.

Don't Tease the Bees

In the morning I went to work with Sam at her Aunt Kathy's bee farm. Sam's mom dropped us off.

Aunt Kathy lived a few miles outside of Glenfield in a small house surrounded by 20 acres. She kept the beehives out back in rows of wood boxes. The entire property was covered with all kinds of flowers. That way the bees had an endless supply of pollen.

After thanking Sam's mom for dropping us off, Aunt Kathy turned her attention to me. "Willie, it's really nice of you to come. I'm sorry I can't pay you for a while. But just as soon as some money comes in, I promise to be generous."

"No problem," I said with a shrug.

"Wonderful," Aunt Kathy replied. She stared at my red hair and even reached out as if to touch it. "You'll be perfect."

As we followed her to the beehives, I pulled Sam aside. "What does she mean, 'I'll be perfect'?"

"Bees can't see the color red. You won't have to worry about getting stung in the head," Sam said with a smile.

"What about the rest of my body?" I asked.

"That's another story," Sam replied.

"You mean a *horror* story," I told her. As we approached the hives, I hugged my arms to my sides, fearful of getting stung. The more I thought about this, the more I didn't like it.

"Willie, as Samantha may have told you, the locusts have driven off my bees," Aunt Kathy explained. "Your job is to draw them back."

"The locusts or the bees?" I asked. "Because what I'd really like to do is catch a trophy locust."

"Well, they were definitely here," Aunt Kathy explained. "But I already got rid of them. Now I just want my bees to come home."

"How nice," I mumbled.

"Willie, my plan is to cover you with bright colors that resemble flowers," Aunt Kathy continued. "As you work your way through the flower beds, the bees will swarm around you."

I looked at Sam. "Tell me this is a joke."

"Sorry," she replied. "Although watching 10,000 bees chase you will definitely be funny."

Locusts. I suddenly loathed their very existence. Instead of making me rich, they were about to get me killed.

"I have a better idea," I countered. "What if Sam gets covered with the bright colors. I'll cheer her on from the safety of the house."

Aunt Kathy shook her head. "Sorry. Sam's experienced with the bees, so she's going to help me with the hives. Your job is basic enough for a beginner."

"In other words, even *you* can't mess it up, Willie," Sam added.

"Oh, yeah? Just watch me. I specialize in messing things up. Besides, how would a bee know if I'm experienced or not? Its brain is too small."

"Do *you* know how to make honey from a bunch of flowers?" Aunt Kathy asked.

I couldn't answer that one, so I did the next best thing. I faked an injury. "Ouch, my foot."

"What happened?" Sam asked.

"Last night I gashed it on a locust shell. Just to be safe, I'd better stay off of it."

"You're fine," Sam said. She turned to her aunt. "He's such a kidder. He's ready to start anytime."

"Wonderful, Willie, I'm glad to hear you say that," Aunt Kathy announced.

"Say what?" I asked. "I didn't say anything. Sam said it."

But Aunt Kathy didn't hear me. Her focus was on her bees, or lack thereof. Not that I blamed her. For all the neatly lined rows of beehives, there was hardly a bee in sight.

Sam's aunt pointed to the edge of her property. "Start out there in the wildflowers. Walk slowly, rustling stems and leaves as you go. As more and more bees attack you—I mean follow you—you'll need to pick up your speed. Oh, and make sure you put that suit on. I wouldn't want you to get hurt."

I looked where she pointed. A heavy white suit—something like a space suit—hung from the shed door. It had a clear hood so I'd be able to see all around. Strips of yellow, orange, pink, and blue material had been tied to the arms and legs.

"Thank You, Lord," I said, glancing to heaven. Making my way to the sting-proof suit, I noticed a plaque hanging next to it. It read: *How sweet are Your words to my taste, sweeter than honey to my mouth! Psalm 119:103.*

"Talk about the perfect verse for a honeybee farm," I said.

"True," Aunt Kathy replied, "but I like this one even better." She showed me a poster inside the shed, far larger than the plaque. It read: *Unless the LORD builds the house, its builders labor in vain. Psalm 127:1.* "It reminds me that success depends on the Lord, not my own selfish desires."

"Good advice, huh, Willie?" Sam suggested.

"Sure," I shrugged, not sure what she was implying. Rather than find out, I changed the subject. "So what's your job today, Sam?"

"My job is to make sure you do your job," she said.

"Oh, that sounds tough," I said sarcastically.

"If only you knew," she replied. "Actually, Aunt Kathy and I will be opening the hives. Aunt Kathy closed them because of the locusts. Once you draw the bees home, they'll see that the locusts are gone and return to their hives, hopefully to stay."

Aunt Kathy drove me to the edge of the property in her pickup. Before I started walking, she tied even more bright ribbons to my suit to help attract the bees. "These colors ought to whip the bees into a feeding frenzy."

"That's a pleasant thought," I said, wanting to run for my life.

"Remember, Willie," she continued, "don't let the bees sting the suit. If they do, they'll die. That's bad for business." With that she returned to the hives.

Standing there, feeling like a man on the moon, I thought of someone with a brain even smaller than a bee's: me. Not only was I missing out on catching a trophy locust, I was about to be a moving target for 10,000 bees. And I couldn't let the bees sting me because of how much harm it would do *them*. And I still didn't know how much I would get paid.

Oh well, here's goes nothing, I told myself. I walked along, kicking the plants around me. I waved my arms like I was trying to flag down an airplane. Soon a few bees began to circle. Then a few more. No problem. They were attracted but not irritated. This would be a cinch.

I could see Sam and her Aunt Kathy opening each hive. Time to start jogging. More and more bees circled around me. It seemed that each flower I bumped into brought along a dozen more bees. The bees buzzed overhead at a safe distance, except for an occasional hot shot that would zip past my face.

This is a breeze, I told myself, *like taking candy from a baby.*

I high-stepped through the daisies like I had just scored a touch down. The buzzing grew louder. I did a little tap dance on a bed of pansies. "Thank you. Thank you very much," I said as the buzzing intensified. The bees formed a black funnel cloud over my head.

"Are you buzzing at me?" I asked, getting cocky. "Go ahead, make my day." I laughed out loud, enjoying the protection of the thick sting-proof suit.

Time to show my stuff, I decided. I weaved back and forth through the rosebushes like I was dribbling a basketball. "He drives. He shoots. He scores!" I announced. "The fans go wild."

The bees continued to zoom in. Talk about success. Aunt Kathy would pay me a fortune for my handiwork. With this suit on, the bees couldn't sting me. As long as I kept moving, they couldn't land to sting the suit. I had it made in the shade. Money in the pocket. What could possibly go wrong?

Rip! The protective suit caught on a thorn.

"No! It couldn't have," I cried. "It didn't."

It did. A sharp thorn had ripped a massive hole in the leg. Immediately, I tried to downplay the significance of the rip. After all, what were the odds of a bee actually finding the …

"Yeowww!" I screamed in agony. A bee had stung my leg. I jumped around in pain, trying to hold the ripped material closed. My frantic movements *really* drove the bees into a frenzy.

If one bee found the opening, how many others would follow? Looking up, I saw a yellow and black attack cloud swirling like a tornado above my head, ready to go ballistic inside my suit. Forget the fancy moves. It was time to run for my life. I felt more like Barney the dinosaur than Carl Lewis.

Waddling as fast as I could in the space-age sting-proof suit, I headed for the house. The bees kept up. Their numbers multiplied. The brightly colored ribbons had whipped the bees into a starving rage. And after getting beat up by the hordes of locusts, they were looking for someone to take out their aggression on—me.

"Ouch!" I wailed as another bee stung my leg. More were lining up for their chance. The hives were too far away. I'd never make it. Then I noticed a pond. It was my only hope. I ran, jumping over flowers, clearing bushes. Almost. I leaped through the air. My hood flew off.

Splash! I sank under the water. Holding my breath, I thought my lungs would burst. *Don't give up*, I told myself. I couldn't surface. Not without a hood. Not yet. I had to hang on.

My eyes bulged. The bad news was, I could feel my heart pounding. The good news was, it was still beating. Had it been a minute? It felt like 10. Finally, I lifted my head out of the water.

Not a bee in sight. I sighed with relief. Then I saw Sam and her aunt standing over me. Sam shook her head. Aunt Kathy just gave me a disappointed look, then surveyed her deserted bee farm.

"Remember how the locusts scared off all my aunt's bees?" Sam asked.

"Yeah," I said.

Sam frowned. "I think you just outdid them."

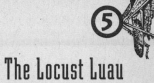

The Locust Luau

After what had happened at Aunt Kathy's earlier in the day, going to the Locust Luau was the last thing I wanted to do. I felt too guilty to enjoy a party. Besides, everyone would be swapping giant locust stories. With a day of competition already gone, I still didn't have a locust to enter in the contest.

But Orville dragged me along anyway. He had decided that since I hadn't earned anything at the bee farm except a jar of honey, I would have to be his personal servant at the luau.

"Willie? My drink! Get it over here now," Orville demanded. He sat at a long table surrounded by other long tables. Each table was full of people laughing and having a good time.

"Yes, sir, your Orvilleness," I grumbled, standing at the drink counter. As Orville watched me over his shoulder, a locust dropped in his stew. He didn't see it. He just kept glaring at me.

"I'm *waiting*," Orville continued. Filling a cup with some punch, I brought it over and sat down next to Orville. As he gulped it down, I eyed his stew. The locust had sunk beneath the surface, out of sight.

I didn't know if I should feel more sorry for Orville or for the locust. I wrote it off as a match made in heaven. In Exodus, God had used locusts to punish the Egyptians for their cruelty to the Hebrews. Because Orville had been mean to me ...

"What are you staring at?" Orville growled. My anticipation betrayed me. I had to quit staring or Orville would get suspicious.

"Nothing," I said. I swallowed a spoonful of stew, hoping that subconsciously Orville would feel the urge to do the same thing.

It worked. While looking over the crowd, Orville scooped up a big spoonful and stuck it in his mouth. His face contorted. The locust must have crawled across Orville's tongue right away.

"Yuck!" Orville gagged. He spat the locust out like a missile. It landed in the hair of the woman sitting across from him, Mrs. Cravits. She had a '50s hairdo that looked like a gray traffic cone perched on her head. The locust didn't stand a chance of escaping that swirled nest. Come to think of it, I'm not sure I could have gotten out of it either.

Once the locust touched her scalp, Mrs. Cravits headed for orbit. She was at least 60, but she jumped higher than a varsity cheerleader. What's worse, she

took off after Orville. I've never seen Orville run so
fast, or a 60-year-old woman who was that quick, for
that matter. In her black orthopedic shoes, she thundered across the turf like a linebacker.

I watched in disbelief, not knowing what to do.
Should I help my older brother before he got
creamed, or should I drop to my knees and laugh hys-
terically? It didn't take me long to figure it out. I
grabbed my ribs and fell to the ground, howling with
laughter. By the time I finally calmed down, I noticed
Amanda standing over me.

"Willie?" Amanda asked. "What are you doing
down there?"

I stood up quickly. "Nothing. Just enjoying the
luau."

"Me too," she said, her face radiant. Amanda
loved social events. "If I could find Bradford, everything would be perfect. Have you seen him?"

"Sorry," I told her.

"Well, if you do, tell him I'm looking for him."
With that she left me, moving gracefully through the
tables and chairs, friendly with everyone. I watched
her go, proud to have Amanda as my sister. She was
one of the most beautiful girls at the luau, but not in
the least bit conceited. If only Orville was as ...

My mind froze. "Oh, no!" I said as I looked up.
Orville resembled a rhino charging me at full speed.
He must have concluded that the locust in the stew

incident was my fault. I didn't know how or why, but I wasn't going to stick around to find out.

The Amazing Amanda

Later that night Amanda asked the family to join her in the living room. That could only mean one thing: talent time. Like all beauty contests, the Beauty Bug Pageant had a talent competition, and the girls went all out.

Initially, the Beauty Bug Pageant was supposed to be for fun, nothing serious. But that was years ago, before Sarah Steele won. Sarah was gorgeous and went on to win the state beauty pageant. After that, every girl in Glenfield grew up dreaming about being crowned Miss Beauty Bug.

Amanda was no exception. She spent weeks getting ready. Appearance-wise, she had a good shot at winning. She had strawberry blonde hair, light green eyes, and a petite nose. She looked more like a doll than my sister. But as for talent ...

My mom and dad exchanged nervous glances as they sat down in the folding chairs Amanda had set up

in the living room. Orville and I sat next to them, feeling queasy. Although Amanda had the looks of a beauty queen, talent was another story entirely.

Suddenly, Phoebe appeared from the hallway.
She was in fourth grade and lived next door. Normally she made a habit of following me around, admiring
my every move. This week she was all Amanda's.

"Ladies and gentlemen," Phoebe announced. "I
present to you the amazing Amanda Plummet."

We clapped, loud and fast, hoping to encourage
her. Amanda stepped into the room wearing black
pants and a tuxedo coat with tails. She looked like a
professional magician. She bowed low.

"For my first trick, I need a volunteer," Amanda
said.

My dad quickly raised his hand. "Pick me," he
called.

"Very well, sir," Amanda replied, nodding gracefully. "Phoebe, please take the gentleman a clipboard." Phoebe handed my dad a clipboard with a
blank sheet of paper on it.

"Now, sir, if you would please write your name
and address on the paper."

My dad felt his pockets for a pen. "Allow me,"
Amanda said. With the quick flip of her wrist, she pro-
duced a pen.

My dad took the pen, which looked kind of
unusual, glanced at it, then pushed it against the
paper. Black ink sprayed all over his white shirt.

"Amanda!" Dad shouted.

A smile spread across Amanda's face. As Dad stared at his shirt in horror, she winked at the rest of us.

"Fear not, sir," Amanda announced, "for with a wave of my hand, the ink will completely disappear."

I stared in anticipation. Talk about a great opener. She really had us going. Maybe Amanda had found her niche as an illusionist. Amanda held her hand in the air. We all watched my dad's shirt. Amanda made a broad sweeping motion, as if brushing aside a curtain.

"Now you see it; now you don't," Amanda proclaimed. But the ink remained.

I glanced at Amanda, hoping this was another one of her tricks. Her confident grin had been replaced by a strange expression, like she was trying to appear confident while in panic mode. She waved her hand again. And again.

"I said, 'Now you see it; now you don't,' " Amanda tried again. The ink looked just as dark. Maybe darker. She took a few steps backward and offered a final wave.

My mom noticed the look of despair in Amanda's eyes and spoke up. "It's okay, Amanda. Some fabrics respond more quickly than others. Just go on to your next trick. I'm sure the ink will disappear soon."

Dad just stared at his shirt. "But, honey, I just bought this shirt for ..."

"It will be fine," my mom said, giving Dad *the look.*

"That's some trick," I admitted. "Spraying your dad's new shirt with ink and not even getting in trouble for it." I started to clap but noticed my mom giving me the same look she had given my dad. With that we all returned our attention to Amanda. As she regained her composure, Phoebe brought out a glass pitcher full of milk.

"Ladies and gentlemen, for my next trick, I need a volunteer wearing a hat."

I reached for my head, thankful to feel nothing but red hair. Off the hook again. Yes! This magic show was getting better all the time. But not for Orville. He was the only one in the room wearing a cap and he knew it.

"This cap is my favorite," he told Amanda.

"That's all right," she said. "It will still work."

Phoebe came over and led Orville to the front of the room. "Please remove your baseball cap and hold it up like a cup," she instructed. Orville reluctantly obeyed and held his cap by the bill above his head.

Taking the pitcher with both hands, Amanda carefully poured the milk into Orville's cap. At least that's what it looked like. When the pitcher of milk was half empty, she stopped and handed the pitcher to Phoebe.

"Now, with three taps of my magic wand, the milk will vanish." Amanda pulled a wand from her coat pocket and after a few theatrical waves, began tapping. "One, two, three. The milk has vanished. You can return the hat to your head."

Orville glanced fearfully at Mom and Dad, his eyes saying, *Please don't make me.* But Dad felt no sympathy, and Mom just cleared her throat and gave Orville *the look.* After a moment of hesitation, Orville plopped the baseball cap on his head. *Splash!* Milk rained down on Orville's face and shoulders. It looked like twice as much as the pitcher would even hold. Orville just stood there, soaked and in shock.

"Bravo!" I cheered. "Instead of making the milk disappear, you made it multiply. Great trick, Amanda. You're a genius." I clapped wildly. "Bravo! Bravo!"

"But it was supposed to vanish," Amanda whined. "This is so frustrating."

"How do you think I feel?" Orville asked. He started to leave, but my mom motioned him back to his chair. Phoebe quickly brought him a towel.

"Maybe I should forget the whole thing," Amanda said, her face downcast.

"No. No. This is fun," I said, glancing at Dad and Orville. "I'm having a blast."

"Well, I guess I can try one more trick," Amanda offered. "It's my grand finale."

"Bring it on," I said, clapping my hands. "More tricks! More tricks! Mom still needs to volunteer. She feels left out." Amanda and Phoebe left the room to get more props.

"Thanks for encouraging your sister," Mom said, patting me on the back.

"It's the least I can do," I said. "I'm just glad I can be so helpful."

At that moment, Amanda and Phoebe returned carrying a table with a large wood box on it. Amanda put her hand in the box while she spoke. "My final trick will produce double the fun. All I need is a brave volunteer."

Amanda stepped back and pulled a saw from the box. "You've heard the song 'Two Hearts Are Better Than One.' Well, today, we are going to find out if that is true. First, I will cut my volunteer in two. Then, with the clap of my hands, I will join the halves together again."

I swallowed hard. The saw looked sharp enough to cut through a petrified forest. I definitely could relate to the petrified part. I did what any quick-thinking person would do—I volunteered my mom.

"Go ahead, Mom," I said. "This is your chance to be a star. Or two stars."

"Actually, Mom won't fit in the box," Amanda said. She extended her hand to me. "Willie, my dear brother, this will be your finest moment."

"More like my *final* moment," I said. "I'm not getting in there."

"What happened to having a blast?" Orville asked, slapping me on the back.

"That was before Amanda wanted to saw me in two. No offense, Amanda, but you're already down two strikes."

At that my mom, my dad, Orville, Phoebe, and Amanda all gave me *the look.*

"Willie, she's waiting," Dad said.

I glanced up long enough to send off a prayer. *Please, Lord, I need a miracle—and fast.*

God is so good. The phone rang. Phoebe picked it up, then covered the mouthpiece. "It's for you, Amanda. It's Bradford."

"Bradford? He wasn't supposed to call," Amanda said. "I didn't have a chance to get ready. I can't talk to him like this. Look at me." Phoebe handed her the phone anyway.

"Hi, Bradford. What a surprise," Amanda said nervously.

From where I sat, it sounded like Bradford was barking like an overprotective Doberman.

"The luau? It was a picnic," Amanda said defensively. "I was just being friendly." More barking.

Amanda narrowed her eyes. "I wasn't flirting because of the Beauty Bug Pageant."

Now's my chance, I thought. "Hey Amanda, see if *Bradford* wants to get cut in two."

"Shut up, you little twerp," Amanda snapped. "No, not you, Bradford. I meant my little brother. Bradford? Bradford?" We could hear the dial tone coming through the receiver. Amanda stared at us through moist eyes.

"What happened?" Mom asked.

"He hung up on me," Amanda cried. She turned and left the room.

I just sat there under the glare of my parents. The razor-sharp saw rested on the table, as if lying in wait. The teeth looked hungry. I wanted to leave, and soon, but feared the saw would come to life and go for my ribs before I reached the door.

Turbo the Tarantula

The following morning I went straight to the lab. The lab is really the back room of my dad's store. Felix and Sam were supposed to meet me for a day of locust hunting. Sam's Aunt Kathy was waiting for a special delivery, so I had the day off. I could use it. With only four days left before the Bug-Off ended, I still didn't have a locust to enter in the contest. But I had a plan.

"Felix, listen to me," I announced, as soon as he arrived. "What I learned yesterday confirms what we learned two nights ago in Shadow Grove: Insects are attracted by what they see. It's a visual thing."

Felix didn't buy my theory. He just wiped his glasses on his shirt and held them up to the light, as if I was wasting his time. "Marvin said he got the mask for a joke," he said. "I believe him. You never saw him wear that locust head when he won, did you?"

"Gimme a break. I was only 8 years old at the time," I complained. "I never even saw Marvin in action."

"That's true. Back then you were probably still at home in diapers," Felix joked.

"Yeah, right. You're really funny," I said. "The point is, we need a mask of our own."

Felix shook his head. "Would you *really* wear a giant locust head to catch locusts?"

"Head?" I laughed. "I'd wear the whole suit. For 5,000 bucks I'd dance up and down Main Street dressed like a giant locust any day."

"Willie, you're too into money."

"It's not about money," I argued, feeling convicted about my attitude. "It's about the Wave Ruler XT, which I'll never get if we don't attract the locusts. It's just like Sam's Aunt Kathy told me yesterday, 'The best way to catch bees is to let them catch you.' "

"What'd you say about my aunt?" Sam asked, suddenly appearing in the back doorway. I explained my plan to her. She not only liked the idea, she convinced Felix to give it a try.

After donning white coats and breaking out our tools, we started. Suddenly, the lab looked more like a mad scientist's operating room than the back room of Plummet's Hobbies. Talk about the ultimate place for an experiment! We had everything we needed to assemble our creation—paint, glue, spare parts, you name it.

To start with, we found a rubber mask of Curly, one of the Three Stooges. His bald head would be perfect. Next we attempted to paint the entire mask locust brown, but the soft rubber kept caving in.

"Felix, we need you to put this on while we paint," Sam said.

"No way," Felix argued.

I took Sam's side. "We're serious. It won't take long." After a little more grumbling, Felix complied. We finished with the brown paint, then Sam started on the details that required fine brushwork, like the nose and mouth.

"Hold still, Felix," Sam ordered.

I studied the mask. "Maybe we should ..."

"Hurry up," Felix interrupted. "I'm suffocating."

"Not now, Felix," I politely informed him. "We're busy." Felix could be really selfish sometimes.

I cut an old eight ball in half to use for the eyes. After a little more gluing and shaping, our creation was complete.

"Ta da!" I said, stepping back.

Sam's expression wasn't very encouraging. "If it doesn't work, we can always try something else."

"It's just the lighting," I explained.

Sam shrugged. "If it's the lighting, let's get him outdoors."

We led Felix outside, then to the park down the street. We found a spot with plenty of trees and bushes that should attract locusts. After placing Felix in a shrub so only his head showed, we stepped back with our nets, ready for the locust frenzy to begin.

Before the locusts could arrive, two little kids came by. I watched their expressions, eager to hear the same admiration for our mask that Marvin Bink no doubt received for his.

"Look at that," one of them marveled. "It looks like Yoda with a suntan."

"May the force be with you, dude," the other replied. Laughing like hyenas, they gave us a thumbs-up sign and walked away.

"Don't let them get to you, Felix. You're a locust magnet," I told him. Searching the sky, I hoped I was right.

But I wasn't right this time. A sun magnet, maybe, but that was it. The direct heat was tougher on the mask than the lighting in the lab. Soon the antennae slid down and stuck straight out from the ears. It looked like someone had shot an arrow through Yoda's head.

"Felix, you're not doing us any good in there," I pointed out. "Can't you even attract one lousy locust before you ruin our mask?"

"What?" Felix snapped. "You try wearing this stupid thing."

"Excuse *me-e-e-e*," I said, lifting an eyebrow. "I guess someone can't handle a little constructive criticism."

"What I can't handle is choking to death." Felix yanked at the neck, trying to pull the mask over his head. But it wouldn't come off. Apparently the high level of toxins in the paint had shrunk the rubber, to say nothing of Felix's brain. Soon he crumpled to the ground, gasping for air.

At that point Sam and I rushed in, knowing our chances of getting a jumbo locust were all but gone. With Sam on one side and me on the other, we grabbed the bottom of the mask and heaved. The rubber barely stretched, but we kept pulling. And pulling.

POP! It finally came off. But I couldn't bare to look. The noise from removing the mask was so loud, I feared Felix's shrunken head had come off with it.

Back in the lab, I tried to reason with Felix. "I know it seems like we failed, but we're really on the right track," I assured him. "You just couldn't appreciate our victory while on the ground gasping for your life."

"How selfish of me," Felix admitted, his voice heavy with sarcasm.

I looked at Sam, hoping to gain her support. "Think about it. What do duck hunters use to attract ducks?"

"Decoys," Sam replied.

"Exactly," I said. "We just need a more convincing decoy. In fact, we need lots of them."

"Willie, we couldn't even make *one*," Sam replied.

"Which is why instead of trying to make them, we'll copy them," I said.

Sam and Felix exchanged a confused look. Then I explained my plan. They thought it had potential. Sam headed for the grocery store, and Felix rode his bike to the library to get the necessary items.

My job was to beg, borrow, or buy a certain remote controlled model from my dad. I found him in the front of the store behind the register.

"Dad, what's our cost on that model?" I asked, edging my way to the glass display case.

"About $25," he said.

"That seems expensive. How do we know it's worth it?" I asked.

"Accuscale makes a good product. I'm sure it's fine," he said.

I shook my head. "But what if it isn't? Just to be safe, I'd better try it out."

"Willie," my dad said, giving me a suspicious look, "what are you up to?"

"Just a little experiment. But don't worry. It will be fine," I promised, removing the model from the glass case. "Then once we know how it works, we can sell it with confidence."

"If you break it, you bought it," Dad informed me, "with or without confidence."

"No problem," I replied. I carried it to the lab and placed it in the center of the operating table. Next, I headed for the boxes of demo hobby pieces in the corner of the lab. After digging past a model boat and a few plane boxes, I found what I was looking for. A dozen Hot Wheels covered the bottom of the box. I removed them and brought them to the lab operating table.

A little while later, Sam and Felix returned.

"Check it out," Felix said. He handed me a stack of papers. Each one had a picture of an enlarged locust on it.

"*Color* photocopies?" I marveled. "How'd you get these? They're awesome."

"What can I say?" Felix replied, shrugging. "Let's just say, I have a few connections at the library."

Makes sense, I thought, considering how smart Felix is. Sam emptied her bag on the table.

"Talk about a farmer's market," I said, equally impressed with her bounty. She had corn, green beans, lettuce, apples, and lots of other fresh produce. The only thing that surprised me was the bag of flour.

"They didn't have actual wheat kernels," Sam said, as if reading my mind. "I figured this would do."

"It's worth a try," I said. "Now check this out." I directed their attention to the center of the operating table. "I give you, Turbo the Tarantula."

Grabbing the remote, I moved Turbo all around. His spider legs moved quickly and silently, just like a real tarantula, only faster.

"Now, let's get to work," I said.

Sam tied strings to the Hot Wheels. Felix cut out the locust pictures and taped them over each car. I located the largest locust photocopy and wrapped it around Turbo so only the legs were visible. I used a rubber band to hold the picture in place. From the top, it looked like a giant locust crawling around.

"Where now?" Felix asked when we finished. "Not to the park again, that's for sure."

"I've got a better idea," I said. "Let's go to the picnic grounds where they had the Locust Luau. That place was thick with locusts."

Felix shrugged. "Sounds all right to me." When Sam nodded with approval, we gathered our locust decoys and a large net, then headed out to catch the biggest locust Glenfield had ever seen.

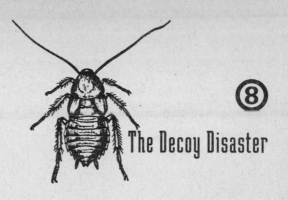

The Decoy Disaster

Compared to yesterday, the picnic grounds were deserted. The tables and chairs were still positioned in rows on the grass. They would be used for the Locust Festival closing ceremony in a few days. The ceremony included a big banquet and the announcement of the Bug-Off winner. We headed for the table I'd sat at during the Locust Luau. It was beneath a large elm tree.

"Time to set up our trap," I said.

Felix positioned the locust decoys on the table and on the ground around it. Sam did the same thing with the fruits and vegetables. She tried to sprinkle the bag of flour evenly over the same area, but it poured out in clumps. It looked like a small range of snow-covered peaks.

I positioned the Turbo Tarantula next to a fresh apple on the ground. Thanks to the photocopy, it looked like a giant locust was enjoying a feast.

"If this doesn't get us a winning locust, nothing will," I said.

We scrambled under the table. Felix and Sam pulled the strings attached to the Hot Wheels to move the locust decoys. With the remote in my hand, I moved Turbo around the apple.

"It makes sense," Felix remarked. "When the real locusts fly overhead and see their buddies down here enjoying a feast, they're bound to drop in."

"Exactly," I said. "And that's when I pounce." I grabbed the net beside me.

Sam and Felix worked the strings, moving the little decoys. I did the same with Turbo. All the while we sat quietly, waiting.

"Take a peek," I urged Sam.

She leaned out from under the table and glanced at the sky. "Nothing yet."

"Don't worry," I told them. "It's just a matter of time." We waited. And waited. Still more waiting. And more.

"Hey Willie, what 'matter of time' did you mean?" Felix asked. "Years?"

"Yeah, Willie," Sam added. "Were you referring to the current Bug-Off or the one five years from now?"

"Quiet!" I said. "I think I hear something." Looking out from under the table, I spotted Mrs. Cravits headed for us. "Get down," I whispered.

When Mrs. Cravits walked within a few tables of ours, she stopped and began searching through the grass.

"What's *she* doing here?" Sam asked.

"She must have lost something at the luau," I reasoned. "She ran like a gazelle. Maybe an earring or a bracelet came loose."

"Or her dentures," Felix whispered. "She was really cooking."

Mrs. Cravits worked her way toward us, carefully picking through the grass.

"Now what?" Sam asked. "No locusts will land with her around. She'll scare them off."

"Not if we scare her off first," I said with a grin. I turned Turbo in her direction. "Check this out."

Turbo crawled through the grass straight for Mrs. Cravits. As he got closer, I moved the remote lever forward to increase the speed. The gears made a high-pitched whirring sound, just like an angry insect.

"Closer," I mumbled to myself. "Stay the course." Turbo closed in.

"Wait until she sees a five-inch long locust coming at her. She'll run for her life," I laughed.

Mrs. Cravits turned toward Turbo but didn't see him. Her eyes were still focused in the grass.

"As soon as she looks up ..." I whispered with anticipation. "Now!"

"AAHHHH!" Mrs Cravits screamed. She turned and bolted, just as she had the other day.

"Good-bye," I waved, feeling confident that I'd overcome the problem. But I waved too soon.

Mrs. Cravits stopped on a dime. She held the strap on her purse like one of those spiked balls on a chain from medieval times. She swung it over her head like a knight ready to attack. Her eyes burned with fury as she charged Turbo. "You disgusting creature!" she shrieked. "I've had enough of your kind!"

"Quick! Reverse!" Felix said, trying to keep his voice low.

I fumbled at the remote, desperate to turn Turbo around. But I was too late. Mrs. Cravits whipped her purse through the air. "Die, bug scum!" she yelled. *Whomp!* The purse smashed to the ground.

I maneuvered Turbo aside just in time. She lifted her purse again. Turbo crawled away, his legs scampering like a blind mouse.

"Hurry!" Sam whispered, shaking my shoulder.

Thump! The purse came down like a wrecking ball. Another narrow miss.

I directed Turbo for the safety of a table, but it didn't work. Mrs. Cravits flipped the table over and swung her purse like an axe.

"Hurry up," Sam pleaded through clenched teeth.

I worked Turbo through the grass, trying to maneuver it to the center of the other locust decoys, the ones on Hot Wheels right by our table. Maybe they would scare off Mrs. Cravits. Wrong again.

Mrs. Cravits charged ahead, reaching the decoys. Her eyes burned like lasers.

"Quick!" I commanded Felix. "Get out there and save Turbo. Be a hero!"

"Hero, schmero!" he said. "I'm not getting whacked by her purse."

"How bad could it hurt?" I asked.

Just then the iron purse connected. A Hot Wheels decoy shattered like a Christmas ornament under a sledgehammer.

"Okay, so maybe it would hurt a teeny bit," I admitted. "New plan: Pull the strings!"

Felix and Sam jerked at the strings to get the decoys out of the way. But they couldn't pull them all to safety. Mrs. Cravits stepped on one of the little cars. It flew out from under her, along with her feet. For a moment she defied gravity. Then it defied her. She came down like a lead balloon. That made her even angrier. Actually, she was furious.

"That's the last straw," she grumbled, climbing to her feet. *Whack! Thump!* Her purse came down again. And again.

After destroying several car decoys, she started for Turbo again. I had no choice. It would never make it to us in time. I gave Felix the remote, then crawled out from under the table.

"It's just a toy," I called out. "Stop! Stop!"

But she didn't. *Slam!* The purse left a crater in the ground. She barely missed.

As Mrs. Cravits lifted the purse up one more time, I reached down to grab Turbo. But Felix kept it crawling in circles. I fell to my knees, groping for Turbo, just as the purse came down. *POOF!*

Good news: Mrs. Cravits missed me and Turbo with her purse. Bad news: She hit a mountain of flour. It exploded in my face like a white volcano. I went blind. I stood up and staggered around until I tripped over a root from the elm tree.

"Sam! Felix!" I shouted. "Save Turbo." *Crunch! Smash! Whomp!* I heard chairs banging, tables falling. It was probably a good thing I couldn't open my eyes.

When I finally did open my eyes, I took one look and closed them again. Turbo was shattered in a million pieces on the grass. The Hot Wheels decoys had been torn from their photocopies. Sam and Felix were hiding behind the elm tree. And Mrs. Cravits was sitting on a chair, gasping for air. She looked exhausted but just as mad. *What if I'm next?* I thought.

Suddenly, Mrs. Cravits bent over and picked up something from the grass. "There you are," she said with a smile. She held up a small gold earring and looked it over for a moment. Then she walked away, as if nothing else mattered.

Felix and Sam came over to me. "Willie, you look like you saw a ghost," Sam said.

"*Saw* a ghost? With all that flour on his face, he looks like one," Felix added. Just then we noticed a rustling in the elm tree.

We watched in awe as Marvin Bink appeared in the upper branches and carefully worked his way to the ground. "That was some spectacle," he said. "Too bad it won't work."

"Don't play dumb with us," I replied. "We know your technique. Just put on the locust head, sit back, and let the big bad bugs come to you."

Marvin laughed. "The mask? I told you that was just a stunt for kids."

"Sure, Marvin, whatever you say," I said. "Just don't try and steal our little brainchild here. As soon as we fix up our decoys, the winning locust is going to zoom in and join his enlarged buddies."

Marvin just shook his head. "Forget the gimmicks, Willie. It comes down to hard work."

I cringed and covered my ears, hoping he wouldn't say it again. But he did.

"It's just hard work."

Aunt Kathy looked me square in the eye. "Willie, I'm afraid it might be even longer than I thought until I can pay you. I spent the last of my money on this bottle of pollen concentrate. Lord willing, it will bring back my bees."

She handed me the bottle. I suddenly felt like Jack holding the magic beans. I tried to hand the bottle to Sam, but she wouldn't take it.

Aunt Kathy took a rag and tied it to a long pole. "Today's plan is similar to the other day's. Sam and I will stay here with the hives. You'll start at the far end of the property. But today, the bees will be drawn to the pollen concentrate. It may have seemed like a lot of bees followed the colored strips tied to your suit last time, but there really weren't that many. Definitely not enough to pay the bills."

"Not enough?" I complained. "They could have flown away with me if they had wanted to."

Aunt Kathy laughed. "I doubt it. But if we're fortunate, today there will be enough for that."

"Fortunate for whom?" I wondered out loud. "Not for me." I looked around for the sting-proof suit, hoping it had been repaired already. I couldn't find it.

Aunt Kathy must have read my mind. "Willie, the sting-proof suit is still damaged, but you shouldn't need it. Not with the pollen concentrate high above your head. At least I *hope* you won't need it," she offered with a laugh. "Now if you'd hurry out there, I'd like to get started."

Get *started?* I'd like to get started for home. Tightening glue caps in Dad's store suddenly sounded like the best job on earth. If only I had taken it while I was still alive.

Carrying the pole and pollen concentrate, I meandered to the edge of the property. I still wasn't sure what to think. If thousands of bees followed the pollen, I could get stung. But if they didn't, I could get zilch—as in, no pay. Talk about an ugly dilemma.

What surprised me was Aunt Kathy's attitude. She had a great outlook, convinced that somehow, some way, the Lord would work things out. If only I could be as positive about the Bug-Off.

The pollen concentrate didn't smell that bad, kind of like flowers and hay with a touch of cinnamon. I doused the rag with the entire bottle.

No spins or jumps today, I decided. I hoisted the pole high in the air, as far away from my unprotected skin as possible.

Taking a few steps, I searched the sky, expecting a yellow and black cloud of stingers. But none appeared.

By the time I walked halfway along the back fence, a few bees began to gather. But today's bees seemed bigger. Much bigger. When I made the turn and walked back across the property, Aunt Kathy took notice. She had a worried look on her face. Looking up, I knew why. Not many bees had gathered.

I decided to shake the pole up and down, hoping to release more of the pollen concentrate into the air. I also kicked the flowers as I went. That helped. A lot. Bees began to swarm in the air above. And what's more, they seemed happy enough with the pollen concentrate to leave me alone, though at times they did get dangerously close to my tempting white skin.

Apparently, Aunt Kathy shared my concern. She disappeared into the house and came out with a pair of binoculars. Reaching the end of the fence, I turned again. The beehives grew closer all the time. "Just stay the course," I whispered to myself.

Suddenly, Aunt Kathy lowered her binoculars and rushed toward me, dodging the flowers as best she could. "Willie," she said, with muffled determination. "Carefully put down the pole and get away as fast as you can."

"Don't worry," I told her, waving the pole back and forth, trying to get the rag to flip like a flag in the wind. "These bees are like pets. They won't hurt me."

"Yes, they will," she warned.

"It's okay," I said, trying to calm her down. "These babies love me. Check it out." I shook the pole up and down. The buzzing intensified, sounding like a high-voltage wire.

Aunt Kathy swallowed and stepped back. "Willie, take a look again. Those aren't bees, they're wasps."

"Wasps!" I choked, freezing in my tracks. "As in unlimited stinging potential?"

"I see you've done your homework," she said.

"Homework? I didn't do any homework! I was only exaggerating so you'd tell me it's not *that* bad."

"Sorry, Willie," Aunt Kathy shrugged. "When you're right, you're right."

"Right? There's nothing *right* about this," I fumed, certain things couldn't get much worse. Boy was I wrong.

Shaking the pole had loosened the rag's knot. With the weight of a thousand wasps, it was ready to fall … on me.

"Just calm down," Aunt Kathy warned. "All you have to do is slowly lower the pole to the ground."

"That's it?" I asked.

"That's it," she said, forcing a grin. "Then run for your life."

Why did I know that was coming? With the lower end of the pole held against my waist, I bent my knees.

"Easy does it," Aunt Kathy said. "Almost there."

Inch by inch, I lowered the pole. More wasps arrived, some hovering over my hair. I squatted down. Only a few more inches until the bottom of the pole touched the dirt.

"Careful," Aunt Kathy whispered to me. "Keep it smooth."

"Whoa!" I gasped, loosing my balance.

Plunk! The pole dropped hard. I let go too soon to steady myself. Looking up, my worst nightmare came true. The wasp-covered rag was falling for my face.

"Run!" Aunt Kathy screamed.

I tossed the pole aside and jumped out of the way. The rag barely missed me. It landed with a *plop!* The wasps zoomed in all directions, but mostly mine.

I sprinted for the house along with Aunt Kathy. The wasps buzzed in pursuit. I swung my arms around my head and ducked, hoping to keep them off.

"We'll never make it!" I shouted. The pond had worked before, why not again? I turned for the water. Aunt Kathy joined me. We hurdled flowers, even rose-bushes covered with thorns.

Aunt Kathy worked hard to keep up. She ran with amazing speed. Apparently running to keep from getting stung went along with bee farming. With the pond only 10 feet away, we leaped into the air like Olympic long jumpers. *Splash!* We made it. The water covered us.

I held my breath even longer than last time. It felt like my lungs would cave in, but I had to hang on. Five. Four. Three. Two. One. I surfaced.

Aunt Kathy was sitting on the bank already, shaking her head. "They must have sent me the wrong hormone. How frustrating."

"Frustrating?" I choked. "It was worse than frustrating. I could have been stung to death!"

"You think that's bad," she observed. "I'm out 50 bucks."

Call me selfish, but that really wasn't the kind of adult sensitivity I was hoping for, especially since I was out at least 50 bucks in pay.

What's worse, the Bug-Off would end in three days. My savings would have to go toward fixing Orville's truck. And I could kiss the Wave Ruler XT good-bye.

The Call of the Wild Locust

That evening at dinner, Amanda made an announcement. "You're all invited to the living room after dinner. There you will enjoy a special sneak preview of my new talent for the Beauty Bug Pageant."

My dad immediately looked down at his white shirt. Orville covered his head.

"Sorry, but I have to floss my teeth after dinner," Dad said.

"And I have to clean my room," Orville added quickly.

"You haven't cleaned your room in years," Amanda said.

"Which is why I need to do it," Orville replied.

All I could think about was my narrow escape from being sawed in half. "No offense, Amanda, but if you cut me in two pieces, I'll be forced to pester you twice as much." Years ago I had stopped annoying Amanda in hopes that her good looks would some-

how rub off on me. When that didn't happen, I
scrapped the idea. I'd went back to my old self and
then some, knowing I had a lot of pestering to make
up for.

"Cut you in two? Silly, Willie, I dropped the illusionist act." Amanda stood up and flipped her hair
back. "After an entire day of rehearsing, I've come up
with a new act that fulfills a lifelong dream of mine.
And because you're my family, you get a sneak preview."

As one we turned toward Mom, wondering what
it could be. Dad and Orville had been at Plummet's
Hobbies all day. I had been at Aunt Kathy's. If anyone
had a clue about Amanda's new act, it would be Mom.
But she immediately disqualified herself.

"Too bad I spent the day at the Glenfield Pavilion
decorating for the Beauty Bug Pageant," Mom said.
"Otherwise, I could have helped you, Amanda."

"That's okay, Mom," Amanda said, standing and
moving toward the living room. "It's more fun if it's a
surprise."

"More fun or more fear?" Orville moaned. A nervous anticipation swept over us. We sat motionless
and stared at our food.

Finally, I took a bite of mashed potatoes and
chewed them. *I am anxious*, I thought. *Who chews
mashed potatoes?* I swallowed hard.

Dad rolled his peas from one side of his plate to
the other. "How much longer do we have?"

"Nine minutes and counting," Orville said, his voice grim.

"Keep me posted, son," Dad said solemnly.

"Stop that," Mom told them. "Amanda needs our encouragement. When we get in there, it's all smiles and applause."

"But, Mom," Orville whined, "my hair still smells like sour milk from her last display of talent."

"Actually, Orville," I put in. "Your hair always smells like sour ..."

Orville grabbed me by the throat. "Unless you want to hand over your savings right now, I wouldn't say a word."

I opened my mouth just enough to gasp for air. Talk about a tough day. No money earned to pay off my brother. No giant locust captured to win the contest. And now I had to sit through another torture session—I mean talent session—with my sister. The Lord was trying to tell me something, but what?

In the living room, we tried to make ourselves comfortable. Mom and Dad sat in their recliners. Orville and I sat on the couch. Soon Amanda appeared wearing a formal black dress. Once again Phoebe was with her, but this time there was no introduction or time for applause. Phoebe simply went to the piano and began to play.

"Wow, she's good," I whispered to Orville. The notes blended together and filled the room like an orchestra.

Amanda moved to the center of the room with her hands clasped in front of her. She lifted her chin.

A recital? I wondered. *Can Amanda sing?* Then again, with Phoebe's beautiful playing, how bad could it be? Ask a silly question ...

It was bad.

When Amanda belted out the first note, I flinched, trying to protect my face from the piercing sound. It was like listening to my dad's Bad Honey record, only worse. Way worse. Amanda sounded like a tone-deaf drowning cat.

"Is this opera?" I whispered to Orville. "I can't figure out the words."

"Do you want to figure out the words?" Orville asked.

"No. But I'd like to figure out what I'm doing here. She should pay me to put up with ..."

"Quiet!" Orville ordered through clenched teeth. "Everything isn't about money. Now quit complaining before I really give you something to complain about."

It was hard to keep a pleasant look on my face when inside I was melting. Amanda wailed and shrieked. An expression of agony came over her face as if she could identify with the words. I could certainly identify with the agony.

"Figaro ..." Amanda crooned. She gestured with her hands. The hairs on the back of my dad's neck stood up, then they fell out. Mom wiped a tear from her eyes. That only encouraged Amanda more, as if she was really moving us.

She was moving us all right ... toward hearing loss.

Orville had sunk into the couch. By turning his head, he was able to cover one ear with the upholstery. *Good idea*, I thought. He just cut his misery in half.

Amanda bellowed and belted in a way no human was meant to sound. Phoebe pounded at the keys.

Time to copy Orville's move. When I turned my head, I noticed something. The window! It was covered with locusts. Glancing around, I noticed that all the windows were covered. Their spiny legs crawled on the glass. And not just any locusts. Big fat ones. Trophies. In other words—money! Someone might as well have taped dollar bills on the glass for me to collect.

No one else noticed. Amanda was too engulfed in her song. Mom and Dad kept their eyes faithfully on her. Orville had gone into a coma. At least that's how he looked with his vacant eyes and drooling mouth.

The locusts continued to arrive. They scurried two deep on the windows. Giants. If I could just get out there with the net, the contest would be mine.

First, I would have to walk past Amanda. She would be hurt, and Orville would hurt me. My mind raced for a solution. I couldn't just sit and watch until the locusts gathered 10 deep. I looked down the hall.

Amanda's singing got louder, like she was moving to a crescendo, the big finale. The window was just a foot or so behind the couch. I had an idea.

I relaxed my arms on the back of the couch. While watching Amanda belt out the notes, I moved my hand to the glass. My plan was simple. I would open the window just enough to let one of the giant locusts inside. With a quick flick, I would knock it to the carpet behind the couch. Once Amanda's song ended, I would get my net and scoop up a $5,000 prize winner. Thanks, sis.

I grabbed the window latch and turned. Exerting a little pressure, I pushed up. Nothing happened. I pushed a little harder. Still nothing.

I glanced over my shoulder. The locusts climbed four deep on the outside of the window. This was my chance. If only the window wasn't stuck.

Keep singing, Amanda, I thought. I jerked harder. My wrist burned. My fingers turned white. My eyes bulged. I heaved with all my strength.

Pop! The window flew all the way open. Locusts poured into the living room. They hopped and crawled across the carpet. They flew from chair to chair. They were drawn to the queen of all locust callers—Amanda. Her voice was like a locust magnet.

"Aaahh!" Amanda screamed. She fell to the ground and covered her head.

Mom joined her, shouting for help. "Get those bugs out of here!"

Orville sprang to his feet and rolled up a magazine. "Bring it on!" he shouted, swinging at them like a major leaguer. He whacked and whacked, launching locusts at the TV. With no singing to attract them, the locusts did an about-face for the window.

"No, no!" I yelled. I pushed down on the window, but now it was stuck open.

Dad picked up a magazine and joined Orville. "Plummet power!" he shouted.

"Gross!" Phoebe wailed. Amanda and Mom remained on the carpet, screaming.

Suddenly, there was a loud knock on the door. "Amanda?" Bradford yelled.

"In here! Help me, quickly." Amanda cried.

The door burst open. Bradford swept into the room like a dashing prince to the rescue. I expected to see a cape behind him. "What's wrong, my darling?" he asked, his face full of concern.

"Bradford, I knew you'd save me," Amanda blubbered. She rose to her feet, only to fall into his arms.

I wanted to gag, but didn't have time. I had to get my net and catch a live locust before Orville and my dad reduced them to pulp.

"Alive!" I shouted. "I can't win the Bug-Off unless I catch one alive."

"Win this," Orville chided. He knocked a plump locust right out the window.

"Home run for Orville," Dad announced. "Who's on deck?" *Whack!*

I ran into my bedroom and came back with my net and a jar, but I was too late. The locusts had either buzzed out through the window or been smashed into the carpet.

"Willie, how rude of you to open the window while your sister was ... um ... while she was ... singing," Dad finally said.

"I couldn't help it," I explained. "Amanda's singing attracted the locusts big time. I saw the jackpot flash before my eyes."

"How dare you say your sister's singing compares to the shrill chirp of a locust!" Bradford said.

"Have you heard her sing?" I asked.

"You little ..." Amanda lunged at me.

Bradford held her back. "It's okay, my darling. He's just an immature child who craves attention."

"Attention? What I crave is cash! As in, five grand for the first-prize locust." I stared at Orville, thinking my debt to him would earn his support. Even he wouldn't cooperate.

"That was so stupid," Orville said.

After more disapproving comments, Amanda and Bradford left the room. Mom and Dad glared. Even Phoebe shook her head at me. Looking beyond them, I dropped my net in despair. *Now what?* I wondered, feeing guilty.

Then I noticed some locusts still flying outside the window. Maybe it wasn't too late after all, but I had to act fast.

Hanging by a Limb

I flipped on the outside lights and ran into the yard. Where were they? I searched the black sky. Some big locusts were still circling our house. I watched for them to come down. Finally, they landed in the big maple tree in our front yard. It was the same tree where I'd almost caught the locust a few days ago when I stood on Orville's truck. This time Orville's truck was parked on the street.

Running to the tree's trunk, I searched through the branches. Locusts by the hundreds crawled on the leaves, chomping them down and chirping to one another.

"Come to papa," I whispered, grabbing hold of a branch. But with my other hand holding the net and jar, I couldn't climb. I put the jar in the back pocket of my jeans and bit the net handle with my teeth.

Grabbing the lowest branch, I climbed the trunk and pulled myself into the tree. The branches were spaced just right for me to reach for one while stepping on another.

I climbed without making a sound, like a panther. The locusts were no doubt oblivious to my presence. I studied the leaves for a giant locust too busy feasting his face to notice me.

Then I saw it. Way out on the end of a branch, resting on a lush green leaf. It looked like something from a sci-fi movie. It was the biggest locust I had ever seen. I watched as it devoured one leaf and started on another.

"You're mine," I promised softly. "All mine." I slithered along the branch like a snake. *Think invisible*, I reminded myself. *You're the new Locust Legend. You're invisible. Only God can see you now.*

Easy. Don't spook it. I glided closer. The branch dipped from my weight. Not too much, though. *No problem*, I told myself. Slide on. Branches can bend to the ground before they break.

I lifted my net, ready to bring it down on the beefy bug. The branch bent more. Almost there. The locust fluttered his wings.

Now! I snapped the net down on the locust. Too hard. The branch snapped.

"Aahh!" I screamed. The branch swung for the ground. I went with it—head first. Then it stopped. I clung to it for my life, hanging upside down. The locust fluttered off with that high-pitched laugh I'd come to know too well.

Now what? I either had to yell for help or turn around before the branch tore loose. Neither option sounded like fun, but I had to act soon. Considering how my family felt about me right now, I decided to solve this one alone.

Then I heard voices coming toward me. They belonged to Amanda and Bradford. They strolled to the trunk of the maple tree and stopped.

Now what? If they looked up and saw me dangling upside down, I'd never hear the end of it. Amanda would tell Orville, who would tell the whole town.

At the Bug-Off ceremony, they would award me "Best Klutz Who Couldn't Catch Anything." No thanks. I'd have to wait it out.

"Your brother wasn't serious, was he?" Bradford asked. "About your voice attracting the locusts? I couldn't imagine dating a girl whose singing attracts bugs."

I waited for Amanda to react. She wouldn't put up with that. She'd tell Bradford to get lost, then belt out a few notes to make sure he left. This was too good to be true. Her singing would drive Bradford away and bring the lunker locusts back to me.

But Amanda didn't say a word. She just stood quietly.

"About this Beauty Bug Pageant," Bradford went on. "In my opinion, the only thing worse than entering a pageant of this nature, is losing it."

"But, Bradford ..."

"Shhhh." Bradford placed his finger on Amanda's lips. She obeyed.

"It's just that I've never lost anything in my life," Bradford went on. "Since I'm not a loser, why would I want to date one?"

That's it, I decided. Time to do something. Nobody calls a Plummet a loser. And nobody treats my sister like that. But what could I do?

Crack!

The Lord provided the answer. The branch snapped loose. I plunged like a maple missile.

"Look out!" I shouted.

Just as Bradford looked up, I came crashing down.

The Munster Mush

The next day I paced around the lab, eager for Sam and Felix to arrive. After last night's near miss, I had a renewed determination to catch a Bug-Off winning locust. And because I was through helping Aunt Kathy, I had the entire day to pull it off.

Not that Amanda would be any help. After Bradford had left last night in a huff, I'd begged and pleaded, but she wouldn't even consider using her voice to help me. But I wasn't discouraged. Thanks to Aunt Kathy, I had an even better idea.

When Sam and Felix walked into the lab, I showed them the blender I had brought from home.

"Here's the deal, guys," I said. "If we're going to win first prize and I'm going to get that $5,000, then …"

"What do you mean *you're* going to get the $5,000?" Sam protested.

"Don't worry, I'll share," I conceded. "The point is, catching a record locust comes down to one word— *concentrate*."

Felix closed his eyes and rubbed his temples. "How's this, Willie? Have you caught any yet?"

"That's not what I mean, Super Spazz. I'm talking about concentrated food, just like Aunt Kathy used to attract the bees."

Sam elbowed me. "Actually they were wasps, remember?"

"That's just because the distributor messed up your aunt's order," I replied. "The idea is still the same."

Sam rolled her eyes. "Since we are already 0 for 2 with these locust-attraction tricks, wouldn't it be better to just work hard and catch a locust the normal way?"

"Whose side are you on—mine or Marvin Bink's? You saw how quickly those wasps arrived. A food concentrate is the key!" I said with conviction. After exchanging a doubtful look, Felix and Sam agreed to give it a try.

"Great," I said. "Now we need to collect the foods locusts like the most and blend them into a concentrate."

"You mean like what we used with the locust decoys?" Sam asked.

"No way," I replied. "That stuff just attracted Mrs. Cravits and that arrogant Marvin Bink."

"What about the locust stew they served at the luau?" Felix suggested.

"Why that?" Sam asked.

"Locusts live for it. Why do you think they call it locust stew?" Felix said, as if the point was obvious.

I tried to control my frustration. "They call it locust stew because of the Locust Festival, not because locusts eat it!"

Sam stood up from the table and paced back and forth, deep in thought. Felix and I watched her, hoping she was on the brink of a breakthrough. Then it hit her.

"Watermelon!" Sam announced. "My neighbors have a garden full of all kinds of fruits and vegetables, but the locusts always go straight for the watermelon."

"Awesome," I said. "That's the break we needed. What else? Just the watermelon?"

Sam thought for a moment. "I think the tomatoes and lettuce go almost as fast, but I'm not sure."

"We'll get some just to be safe," I decided. "How much money do you guys have?"

"None!" Sam and Felix replied in unison. "This is your idea. You buy the stuff."

I shook my head. "I don't want to dip into my savings, especially since I might need it to repair Orville's truck." Then another idea hit me. "Sam, why can't we get this stuff from your neighbors' garden?"

"Can't hurt to ask," she said. "They've always been eager to share." With that we left the lab on a fresh produce hunt, determined to create the first-ever locust food concentrate.

As we approached Sam's house, Felix began to fidget like he was uneasy. I found out why soon enough.

"Sam, we're not going to the Munsters' house, are we?" Felix asked.

"Yeah, how'd you know?" Sam replied.

"I didn't," Felix said. "I just feared the worst."

Sam's neighbors really weren't the Munsters. In fact, she hated it when we forgot and called them that. But because this older couple lived in a dreary old mansion that sat on a big corner lot, the kids of Glenfield called them the Munsters after the famous TV family.

Their real name was Spiff, which didn't fit their house at all, or their appearance for that matter. The Spiffs had bony faces and yellow teeth. I had only seen them once when they yelled at Felix for cutting across their lawn.

When we arrived, Sam knocked on the front door, but nobody answered.

"Now what?" Felix asked.

"Maybe we should call it off," Sam suggested.

"No way," I protested. "Let's just go through the side gate. You said they were eager to share."

"Yeah, but we should ask first at least," Sam argued.

"I agree," I said, urging Sam toward the gate. "But they're not *here* to ask. Look, as soon as the Munsters come home, you can explain what happened. I'm sure they'll understand."

Reluctantly, Sam agreed. When we got to the gate, it was locked.

"No problem," I said, stepping on a planter box. "We can hop this fence in no time." I pulled myself up and dropped down on the other side.

"Willie, I don't think this is such a good idea," Sam said, still outside the fence.

"Maybe not," I said, getting frustrated. "But right now it's the best idea we've had. Now hurry up." When Felix and Sam finally hopped over, we crept along the side of the house to the garden.

"No wonder the locusts like it here," I said. "This place is the mother lode of all fresh produce." I surveyed the rows of big vegetables and bright fruit.

"Let's just find what we need and get out of here," Sam told us. "I feel like we're stealing."

"Me too," Felix said. "And I'm already on the Munsters' bad side."

"It's not Munster, it's Spiff," Sam reminded us.

"Let's just hurry," I ordered. "The sooner we get back to the lab, the better." We gathered up a watermelon, two plump tomatoes, and a head of lettuce. A few ears of corn, some broccoli, and a zucchini squash were also thrown in, just to help entice the locusts. That's when the sprinklers came on.

"Hit the dirt," Felix yelled. He dove for the ground but landed face first on a sprinkler.

"I think someone's seen too many war movies," I told Sam. We clutched all the produce and stumbled along the backyard fence. Climbing to his feet, Felix chased after us.

We arrived at the gate drenched, but at least we were out of the sprinklers' range. Sam removed her backpack and we stuffed what we could inside. The watermelon wouldn't fit, though, and the tomatoes could get smashed and ooze all over. Then we heard a group of girls in the street playing jump rope.

I started to climb back over the gate, but Sam grabbed me. "Where are you going?"

"Back to the lab. Remember?"

"Not with those girls out there. If they see us hop the fence with this stuff, they'll think we stole it. Then they'll tell the whole neighborhood. While we're at the lab, the Spiffs will find out and I'll be dead."

"But you're going to tell them anyway," I said.

"I know," Sam fumed. "But they should hear it from me, not from someone else. Not that I would even be in this mess if you hadn't talked me into it."

"Relax," I said. "It's for a worthy cause."

"What worthy cause?" Sam asked. "So you can win $5,000? Sounds more like a *wealthy* cause to me."

"If it's a wealthy cause, it is a worthy cause in my book," I laughed.

Sam's eyes filled with rage. "No wonder the Bible says the love of money is the root of all evil. Ever since this contest started, you've been a greedy, selfish pain-in-the-neck."

"Okay, okay. I was only kidding," I said, trying to calm her down. "Don't worry. I've got an idea to get us out of here. Felix, lift up your shirt."

"Forget you," he said, clamping his arms around his waist.

"Come on," I prodded.

He looked at Sam, then grudgingly did as I asked. Getting behind him, I lifted his shirt and slid the watermelon up to his neck. To keep it from falling back down, Felix hunched over.

"Oh, that's cute," Sam said sarcastically.

Ignoring her, I placed a tomato on each of my biceps. My sleeves held them in place.

Felix could barely see me because he was hunched over like that, but when he finally did look up, he had a fit.

"Oh, that's not fair," Felix whined. "You look like Superman and I look like the Hunchback of Notre Dame." Felix tried to keep eye contact while he spoke, but the weight of the watermelon kept him doubled over. I wanted to encourage him, but he really did look like a hunchback.

"Don't worry, Felix," Sam said. "No one's going to say anything."

Since Felix was the heaviest, we started with him. We boosted him to the top of the fence. That's when we heard the screams from the street.

"It's the Hunchback of Notre Dame!" the girls shrieked. "He moved in with the Munsters." We heard more screams, followed by the scampering of feet. The girls were scared to death. Not that I blamed them. Felix did look kind of scary.

"That's it!" Felix grumbled. He tried to fall back on our side, but we wouldn't let him.

"At least they didn't call you Cousin Itt," I said.

"Why would they? That's the Addams Family," he replied.

We pushed Felix until he dropped down on the other side. Then Sam and I climbed over to an empty street.

"See, Felix, everything happens for a reason," I said with a smile. "The girls were so disgusted by your hideous appearance that they ran away. Now Sam and I can leave without being seen. Doesn't that make you feel special?"

"I'll show you special," Felix said, lunging for my throat. Fortunately the watermelon kept him from reaching it.

"Hurry," Sam insisted, "before the girls return with their parents."

We ran down the street and cut through the alley toward the lab. Sam led the way, followed by Felix. I took the rear guard. Reaching the park, we worked our way through the trees. Then I heard a whistle and turned to look. It was a group of high school girls watching me.

"Nice arms," one of them said. Felix was right. I did look like Superman.

"Willie 'Superman' Plummet, at your service," I announced, making my voice sound deep and suave. I raised my arms and flexed my biceps. The tomatoes bulged in my T-shirt. The girls clapped and whistled. I loved it. I spun and posed like a bodybuilder. More applause.

I turned my back so the girls could see my biceps from another angle. All at once the cheering stopped. What happened?

Turning around, I found out. The girls' boyfriends had arrived, and clapping was the last thing these guys had on their minds. They were coming straight for me, fists clenched.

So much for Superman. I lowered my arms, swallowed my pride, and ran.

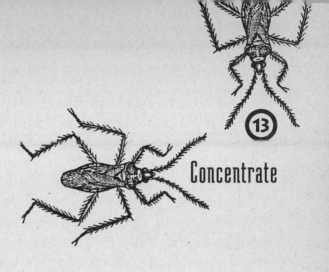

13

Concentrate

The safety of the lab never felt so good. As soon as I ran through the door, Sam locked it behind me. We spread the vegetables on the table. I added the tomatoes and we started cutting everything up. We dumped all the chopped stuff into the blender and hit "liquify."

"Now we're getting somewhere," I said. The watermelon, tomatoes, lettuce, and other vegetables swirled in the blender's glass pitcher. We shut it off and lifted the lid. The juice smelled delicious.

"Forget the locusts," Sam said after trying a sip. "This is for me. It's excellent."

"For five thousand bucks you can have all you want," I told her. "Otherwise, it's reserved for the contest-winning locust I'm about to catch."

"Money again," Sam muttered. "Why am I not surprised?"

Although the drink was good, it still wasn't concentrated. We drained the water by pouring it through a strainer, then returned the pulp to the blender.

"One more ingredient and we're all set," I informed them. Grabbing the jar of honey Aunt Kathy had given me, I poured the whole thing into the blender. After turning it on, I let everything whirl around for a few minutes, then shut it off.

"Wha-la," I said, removing the lid. A delicious aroma filled the room. It was all we could do not to polish off the concentrate ourselves.

"I'm impressed," Felix said. He took a big whiff and smiled.

"Now we just need something to keep this stuff in," I said.

When nothing turned up in the lab, Sam and Felix checked some nearby Dumpsters in the alley. They returned with an empty shampoo bottle.

"How about this?" Sam asked. "It was behind Pearl's Beauty Supply. This is the most expensive shampoo you can buy."

"Nothing but the best for our locust concentrate," Felix added.

We poured the concentrate into the shampoo bottle and shook it up.

"It's show time," I said. After gathering our gear, we headed off again. On the way to test our locust formula, I couldn't resist stopping at Glenfield Water Sports to stare at the Wave Ruler XT in the window.

"You will be mine," I promised, leaning so close my breath fogged the glass.

"Can we go now?" Felix complained.

I waved him off. "This is a special time for me and the XT. Give us a minute."

"Willie, look!" Sam said, jerking my arm. She seemed surprised.

Turning around, I knew why. Aunt Kathy was carrying her sting-proof suit into the pawn shop.

"Didn't she just get that fixed yesterday?" I asked.

"Yep," Sam replied. "She must be selling it to pay her bills. I guess she's calling it quits on bee farming."

"How sad," Felix said. A few minutes later Aunt Kathy left the pawn shop, empty-handed.

"Bummer," I said. "Oh well, let's go. We have a giant locust to catch."

"Nice compassion," Sam said sarcastically. "There must be something we can do to help her."

"It's worth a try," Felix said.

Sam nodded and went into the pawn shop. I turned my attention to the Wave Ruler XT until she returned.

"Here's the deal," Sam said. "We can buy the suit back for my Aunt Kathy for one hundred dollars."

"I'll help," Felix said. "But all I have is $20."

"I can come up with that much," Sam offered. They both looked at me.

"Forget it!" I said. "That's sixty bucks for me to pay. And I still haven't fixed Orville's truck."

"Come on, Mr. Scrooge. You can afford it," Sam said. "And besides, if our locust food works as well as we think it will, a protective suit might come in handy. I wouldn't want to get caught in the middle of a locust feeding frenzy."

"We'll be all right," I said. "And that suit isn't going anywhere. As soon as I win the Bug-Off, I promise to buy it back for Aunt Kathy. Now let's go."

At Shadow Grove we soaked a rag with our locust attractor. Then we tied the rag to a long stick. I told Felix to do just what I had done with the pollen concentrate at Aunt Kathy's. I walked next to him, ready with my net. Sam sat on a stump and watched us, still stewing over her aunt's problem.

Fifty yards later, only a couple of small locusts had appeared. They nibbled a little, then flew off. Several more followed them, but none of the locusts were big enough to bother with.

Weaving through the thick trees, we worked our way back to Sam. Felix waved the rag, hoping to release the concentrated aroma. It didn't help.

"Felix, this is a repeat of your mask performance in the park," I said, trying to motivate him. "Now get it together or you're fired."

"Fired? I quit!" Felix threw the stick down and joined Sam on the stump.

I considered waving the rag myself but decided why bother? Dropping my net, I vented my frustration. "This has been the worst week of my life. Everything's going wrong!"

"What do you expect?" Sam asked. "You've been too greedy and selfish—all you think about is winning that money."

"Selfish?" I scoffed. "I helped your aunt when I could have been catching locusts."

Sam just rolled her eyes at me, as if I was beyond help. For a while no one spoke. I just stared at the ground, feeling miserable. Sam was right and I knew it.

"There's one last thing we can try," Felix said. "Sometimes chemicals need heat to react with one another."

"Meaning?" Sam asked.

"Think about it," Felix continued. "When do brownies smell the best? When your mom mixes the batter, or when they're hot from the oven?"

"The oven," I said, feeling a glimmer of hope. "So all we have to do is cook the concentrate."

Felix shook his head. "If we cook it, we might steam off too much aroma. Better to slowly warm it overnight. Just place the bottle against a hot water pipe."

"I know the perfect spot," I said.

14

Shampoo Blues

I spent the next day working at Plummet's Hobbies. My dad needed me to reorganize the model
planes and I needed to pay for the Turbo Tarantula. I
still hadn't earned a dime working for Aunt Kathy, and
my chances of winning the Bug-Off were getting
increasingly slim. If I didn't make some money soon,
I'd have to use my savings to repair Orville's truck.

All day I thought about our locust food concentrate. I couldn't wait to get home and try it out. Maybe
our water heater trick would really work.

At 4:30 P.M. I left the store and rode straight home.
Going into the bathroom, I opened the cabinet
beneath the sink. The bottle wasn't there. I checked
around. I had left it right next to the hot water pipe,
but it was gone.

"Now what?" I asked. I ran to the phone and
called Felix, thinking he had tried it out himself.

"Where's the locust concentrate?" I demanded as soon as he answered.

"You had it," he said, getting defensive. "But if you want, I'll come over and help you look for it."

"Fine," I said, then hung up to call Sam.

"Sam's not here," her mom explained. "She's helping her Aunt Kathy box up the bee equipment. I'm afraid her aunt is calling it quits on bee farming."

"Bummer," I said, feeling bad. But I had to stay focused. "Sam didn't have an expensive bottle of shampoo with her, did she?"

"Not that I know of," Sam's mom said. "But I'll have her call you when she gets home."

Hanging up, I ran through the house, yelling for anyone.

"What? What?" Mom asked, coming downstairs.

"There was an expensive bottle of shampoo under the bathroom sink," I explained. "Have you seen it?"

Mom thought for a moment. "I may have seen your sister with a new bottle of ..." I didn't wait for my mom to finish. I returned to the bathroom. Amanda couldn't have. She wouldn't have.

She had.

The bottle of shampoo stood in the corner of the shower. I picked it up. It was half empty. Amanda had found it in the cabinet and used it to get ready for the Beauty Bug Pageant. It made sense. On the biggest night of her life, she would want to use the best shampoo money could buy. Too bad her hair was really full of locust attractor.

With all the honey mixed into the concentrate, it's a wonder she could even rinse it out. Then again, maybe she didn't. I crumbled to the ground, not knowing if I should laugh or cry. Then I heard my mom coming down the hall. I quickly stood up.

"Did you find the shampoo?" she asked, coming into the bathroom.

"Yeah. Right here," I said, holding up the bottle. "Have you seen Amanda?"

"She already left for the pageant. The contestants have to arrive three hours early to rehearse and get ready." My mom looked at the bottle. "So what's with the shampoo?" she asked.

Just then the doorbell rang. Perfect timing. "I'll tell you later," I said, running downstairs to get the door.

It was Felix and Sam. I led them straight to my room and explained what had happened. They just stared at me with their jaws on the floor.

"It's unbelievable," I went on. "And terrible and horrible and ..."

"How sweet," Sam interrupted, "that you're so concerned for your sister."

"I'm not just concerned. I'm furious. How can I get a prize-winning locust with only half as much con-centrate?"

Sam shook her head. "Why am I not surprised?"

When we arrived at Shadow Grove, it felt even creepier than normal, like an eerie quiet held everything captive. We even found ourselves whispering.

"Just a little more ought to do it," I said softly. Squeezing the shampoo bottle, I covered the rag with locust concentrate. A delicious aroma of honey and watermelon filled the air. Our setup was similar to yesterday's. The wet rag was tied to a long pole, then lifted into the air.

I turned my attention to Felix. "Here's the plan. You need to lift the pole way up there and keep it moving. We want the aroma of the concentrate to catch in the breeze. I'll be ready with the net. Sam will stand by with the containers."

"Then what?" Felix asked.

"As soon as the Bug-Off locust arrives, lower the pole, and I'll take care of the rest," I told him.

"What if something goes wrong?" Felix asked.

"What could possibly go wrong?" I replied.

"Nothing, if we had brought the sting-proof suit for him to wear," Sam put in. She glared in my direction.

Without responding, I turned my back on Sam and spoke to Felix. "Just keep the rag moving through the trees. I'll follow along, just out of sight. That way I won't spook the locusts."

Felix set off through the trees. He walked slowly at first, but nothing appeared. He trekked a little farther. Nothing, not even a few little locusts like we had attracted the other day.

"Shake the rag more," I told Felix. "You need to release the aroma." Felix shook the rag back and forth, up and down. Still nothing.

"That's some locust attractor," Sam teased, staying on my heels.

Felix continued to weave through the trees, holding the rag up like one of those medieval banners that knights carried into war. But this was no war. Desertion, maybe, but definitely no war.

I studied the branches that formed a black canopy over us. There wasn't a bug in sight. Shadow Grove was desolate.

"Sure, just warm the stuff overnight so the chemicals can gel," I complained in Felix's direction. "What a joke." I stopped in my tracks, not wanting to go any farther. Sam stopped with me. But Felix kept walking away from us. "Let him go," I mumbled.

Then I heard a faint whirring in the distance, like a model airplane, only larger. I grabbed Sam's arm so she wouldn't move.

"What's that?" she asked, looking around. We stood motionless, listening. A feeling of dread filled my stomach. The whirring drew closer and came from the sky. But with all the thick branches blocking our view, we couldn't see anything.

The whir became a loud buzz, like the world's largest power line ready to explode. When it reached the far side of Shadow Grove, I recognized the sound. It could only be one thing: brown out! Locusts by the hundreds of thousands on the attack.

I didn't know what to do. This was my chance to catch a trophy. But what would happen to Felix? Would the locusts attack him too?

Sam must have read my mind. "We need to warn Felix! The locusts might eat him alive."

I thought about the prize money. "That's a chance I'm willing to take," I told Sam.

"Well, I'm not!" She ran past me. "Felix! Drop the rag! Quick!"

But Sam was too late. Like a brown tornado, the locusts dropped through the branches, devouring everything in sight.

Felix tossed aside the rag and tried to escape, but the locust tornado swallowed him too. They buzzed like an insect army, like the bugs you read about in Revelation.

"Felix!" I shouted. I charged ahead and caught up with Sam.

"Felix!" we both screamed. We approached the locust tornado, still unable to see Felix. The locusts had taken him hostage.

"If we don't get to him soon, he'll be cocoon food by morning," I said.

We squinted and waved our arms in the air, just a few feet from the brown wall of locusts.

"Let's do it!" I screamed. Sam and I charged into the center of the locust cloud. Locusts smacked into us from all sides. Some clung to our clothes and bit hard. We slapped them off while desperately searching for Felix.

"There!" I said, pointing at the ground. The pole and rag were on the ground, completely covered with locusts. But there was no sign of Felix.

"What's that?" Sam asked. She pointed to a stump.

Batting the locusts from my face, I ran to the stump. It looked like Felix's shirt, but I couldn't tell if he was in it or not. It was covered with too many locusts.

"Felix!" I shouted, but the shirt didn't respond.

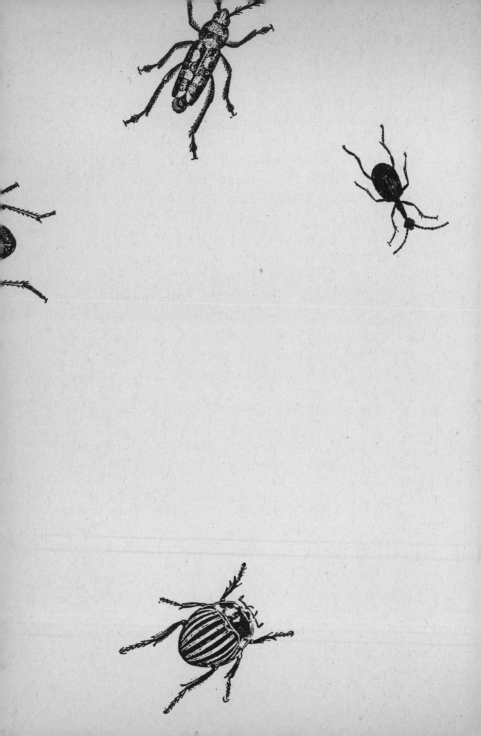

15

The Beauty Bug Brown Out

Like a locust tornado Sam and I stepped around the stump, yelling for Felix with each step. We reached the edge of the locust cloud. We could see a little farther. There was a stream in front of us. We ran to it and found tracks. We waded into the water.

"Felix! Where are you?" Sam shouted.

"Are you alive?" I yelled. We splashed through the shallow water. Mud clung to our shoes. Then we spotted him.

Felix was lying on the bank up ahead, face down. We ran to him and turned him over. His eyes were closed. His mouth was bulging. I leaned close to his face to see if he was still breathing.

"He may need mouth-to-mouth," Sam urged.

"Anything but that," I begged, cringing.

At that, Felix spewed a mouthful of water in my face.

"Serves you right," he said. He sat up and rested his head in his hands. "I could have been killed."

Felix was right. My greed had almost cost my best friend his life. Rather than make a wisecrack, or dish out the perfect comeback, I kept my mouth shut. I sat in silence, feeling guilty, *really guilty*, not just for refusing to buy the sting-proof suit, but for my attitude all week. Before I said another word, I closed my eyes and asked God to forgive me. Then I helped Felix to his feet and asked for his forgiveness too.

"I guess so," he said, still mad about the locust attack.

I couldn't blame him for his less-than-whole-hearted answer. Considering what a jerk I'd been, he probably didn't know whether he could trust me. I apologized again, to both Felix and Sam, determined to show them how bad I felt.

Then we turned toward Felix's shirt and once again dropped our chins in awe. Just as quickly as the locust tornado had arrived, it swirled up through the trees and out of sight.

"Where do you think it's heading?" Sam asked.

"I hope it's as far away from here as possible," Felix replied.

I thought for a moment, then swallowed hard. "I think ... I know."

"Where?" Sam asked.

"The Beauty Bug Pageant," I suggested with dread. "To find Amanda. She used half the bottle of locust concentrate on her hair. Remember?"

"But she used it for shampoo. She must have rinsed it out," Sam replied.

Felix shook his head. "This stuff doesn't rinse out. Not with all the junk we put in it."

"We have to help Amanda before it's too late," I said, wiping the cold sweat from my forehead. I explained my plan, then the three of us took off in three different directions.

When I arrived at the Beauty Bug Pageant, my side ached from running the whole way. I doubled over with my hands on my knees. I gasped for air. The pageant was well underway. All the contestants and spectators had arrived, but so far the locusts hadn't.

There was still time. Straightening up, I made my way to the door.

"Ticket, please," the usher said.

"I don't have a ticket," I told him.

"Then you can't get in."

"But my sister's in the contest," I argued.

"Good for her. But you still can't get in without a ticket." He closed the glass door. I wanted to scream. Time was running out. The locusts could arrive any second. But how could I explain that to the doorman? He'd just laugh in my face.

I listened for the wind. Nothing. Just dead quiet, like Shadow Grove before the insect tornado hit. I had to do something fast.

Walking around the brick building, I saw the situation go from bad to worse. The upper windows of the pavilion were open. The screens looked like they would fall apart at the slightest touch. The locusts could burst through in a flash.

I paced back and forth, waiting on Felix and Sam. "Where are you guys?" I moaned.

I watched the sky and listened. Still no locusts. Then a girl's voice boomed over the microphone. One of the contestants was showing off her talent.

"But seriously, folks," she said, "the other day a guy asked me for some spare change. He said, 'I haven't had a bite in days.' So I bit him."

The girl laughed at her own joke, but she was the only one. The audience was silent. It was quieter in there than out here. Then it occurred to me. I'd never heard what Amanda was going to do for *her* act. My poor sister. First she'd bomb on stage, then the locusts would eat her alive.

I looked down the street for any sign of Sam and Felix. "Please, God," I prayed. "Get them here in time."

A man's voice boomed over the loudspeakers. "Ladies and gentlemen, our final contestant is the lovely Amanda Plummet. Her talent for the evening will include a piano selection by Johann Sebastian Bach."

A polite applause filled the pavilion, followed by silence. Then the announcer came on again. He sounded pleasantly surprised. "Wait a minute. I have just been handed a note. There's been a last-minute change." *What kind of change?* I wondered. Had Amanda sensed the coming danger and withdrawn? Had someone warned her? This could be good news.

The announcer continued. "In recognition of Glenfield's Locust Festival, Amanda will be performing, 'Chirp of the Wild Locust.' "

"What?" I choked. "That's not good! That's bad! Very bad!"

I pounded on the brick building, wishing they could hear me. I screamed at the windows high above. "Don't do it, Amanda!"

I searched the sky, my eyes bulging with dread. Between the locust concentrate in Amanda's hair and her shrill voice blasting over the microphone, she was a locust magnet. A dead locust magnet. Locusts would come from around the globe. She didn't stand a chance. And neither did anyone else in the auditorium. The tornado of ravenous locusts would level the place.

I ran along the building, desperate to find a way inside. I had to warn Amanda. I came to a door on the side of the pavilion. It was locked. I pounded and waited. No answer. I pounded again. Nothing. I started to leave. Wait! Was that someone coming to the door?

I put my ear against the door. Was it coming from inside? Maybe someone was coming to unlock the door. I listened. Wrong again.

The sound was coming from the sky—the power line buzz of a million locusts on the move. The brown tornado had returned. I couldn't see it in the dark. But it was up there and descending fast.

I pounded on the door again. "Let me in," I begged.

"Hey!" a voice called from behind me.

I ducked down, fearing it was the usher.

"Willie," the voice called again. Suddenly Sam and Felix appeared. Sam had the sting-proof suit rolled up under her arm.

"You got it!" I said.

"The guy at the pawn shop was just leaving," Sam explained, "but I stalled him until Felix arrived with your savings."

"It felt weird taking the money from your room without you there," Felix added.

"No problem," I said. "We can handle weird. It's a million ballistic bugs that I'm worried about. Now let's get this suit on Amanda before it's too late."

"I'm afraid it is," Sam said.

Amanda's locust imitation echoed from the sound system. Her shrieking and chirping filled the night air. Seconds later, the first locusts arrived. They smashed into the screens overhead, determined to get inside.

"We need to find a way inside," I shouted. Running along the building, we turned the corner and found another door. More locusts arrived, chirping and dive-bombing our heads.

Boom! Boom! Boom! I pounded on the door. My knuckles turned white, but I kept at it. "Let us in!" I shouted.

Felix batted at the air, trying to defend us from the tornado of locusts. It was a losing battle. The great and horrible bug brown out had come.

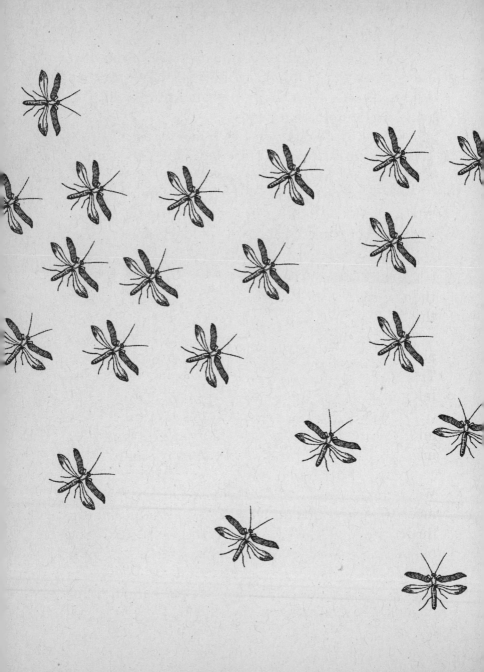

16

Bradford's Bad Hair Day

Locusts by the thousands shot past our faces at the speed of sound. They scratched our skin with their spiny feet.

"Willie, up there!" Sam pointed to a window above the door. It was open and didn't have a screen. The locusts saw it too and began to pour in. I had to hurry.

"Quick!" I yelled. Felix and Sam gave me a boost and I pulled myself through. Once I had squirmed inside, I dropped down and unlocked the door.

"Hurry," I ordered, waving Sam and Felix inside. We slammed the door and the window above it so no more locusts could get inside. We worked our way through the backstage area, past the dusty props and old pieces of scenery. We could hear the locusts gathering outside, buzzing with excitement. They were almost as loud as Amanda's locust call blasting through the speakers.

Soon we came to the other contestants waiting offstage. They were covering their ears. I couldn't blame them. Amanda's shrieking and chirping was deafening.

Then a security guard noticed us. "What are you doing here?" he barked. "Contestants only."

He came right for us. We took off, dodging contestants and jumping props. I weaved through the curtains and caught a glimpse of Amanda on the stage. She looked stunning in her dress. But even more stunning were the upper windows that wrapped around the auditorium. They were brown with locusts. Any second the screens would tear open and locusts would pour into the pavilion like water over a dam.

"Come here!" the security guard called. He grabbed at me, but I dodged out of the way and wrapped myself in another curtain offstage.

"Nice try," I chuckled. This guy couldn't catch me if his life depended on it. Or so I thought. He tackled me from behind like a linebacker, sending us both sprawling across the stage.

Amanda tried to ignore us, determined to finish her act. She chirped higher. Louder. That did it. The screens gave out.

Locusts by the thousands burst through the windows. They poured down on the audience. Children screamed. Ladies screamed. Even the men screamed.

The locusts descended on Amanda like a funnel cloud. She tried to run but tripped over me and the security guard.

"Sam," I yelled, desperate to get the suit on Amanda. No answer. Had the security guard thrown Sam out?

I rose to my knees and batted away the first locusts to reach Amanda.

"Sam," I yelled again. Suddenly she appeared with Felix.

"Put this on! Quick!" I ordered Amanda, handing her the suit. Locusts dropped in her hair. We picked them out as she slipped into the white coveralls. Sam helped her put the suit on and Felix and I swung at the locusts.

But the main battering ram of locusts was yet to come. It hovered in the air, gathering strength.

"Hurry up," I said. "Here it comes!" The battering ram zeroed in. Closer. Closer. Amanda pulled on the hood and zipped up the suit.

Wham! The locust tornado knocked her to the ground. Sam and Felix crawled for the safety of the stage curtain. I stayed on the stage, covering my head, so thankful that Amanda was safe.

The buzzing intensified. Screams filled the pavilion. Locusts swooped down and pulled at my shirt, as if to take me with them. I couldn't bare to look.

Then I heard the voice of a woman. A familiar voice.

"You disgusting vermin," the voice hollered, challenging the locusts. "Take that!" Peeking through my fingers, I couldn't believe my eyes. It was Mrs. Cravits, onstage, swinging her purse with righteous fury. She smacked locusts from one side of the pavilion to the other.

But she couldn't handle them all. One got past her purse and bit her, then another. That was enough for me. Enough of this cowering on the floor stuff.

"Bring it on," I shouted, grabbing the Beauty Bug trophy from the judges' table. Taking a stand next to Mrs. Cravits, I started swinging. "You want some of this?" I challenged, rocketing a locust off the back wall. I unleashed a week's worth of locust frustration in each swing. "Fore," I said, hitting one off the stage. Mrs. Cravits and I kept swinging until the tide shifted.

"Take that," she exclaimed, walloping a locust toward the ceiling. Soon the locusts retreated through the upper windows. They poured out just as quickly as they had entered.

"Yes!" I said, giving Mrs. Cravits a high five.

After a few minutes the locusts were all gone, except for a small swarm devouring one of the guys in the audience. I took a closer look. It was Bradford. His thick, princely hair looked like beard stubble.

I turned to Amanda. "You didn't lend him some of the locust shampoo, did you?"

She nodded. "Bradford likes anything expensive. On the way here, I dropped some by for him to try."

Amanda made her way toward him, still wearing the
protective suit. She waved off the remaining locusts.
I helped, knowing I would have to explain. But Bradford wasn't satisfied with my explanation—or my
apology.

"The worst thing that ever happened to your sister is *you*," he snapped. Then he turned to Amanda.
"Didn't I order you not to try that degrading locust
chirp? You've embarrassed me for the last time. We're
finished!"

I stared at Amanda, expecting her to defend me,
or at least herself, but the announcer didn't give her a
chance.

"Ladies and gentlemen, please take your seats,"
he stated. "The judges have selected a winner. If we
can have the finalists onstage please."

Amanda joined the other girls onstage. The pavilion grew quite. Everyone stared as the mayor walked
to the podium and opened the envelope.

"And the winner is ..." the mayor said, pausing
for effect, "Miss Amanda Plummet."

Applause filled the pavilion. The audience gave
Amanda a standing ovation. Mom and Dad stood in
the front row, beaming. Phoebe and Felix were next
to them, clapping wildly.

Still wearing the suit, Amanda stepped forward to
receive the crown. Before she did, she lowered her
hood. It was a beautiful moment, like an angel had
just been unveiled. When the ceremony was over, we

all rushed onstage to congratulate her. Bradford wasn't far behind, but his tone sure had changed.

"Darling, I knew you could win," he said, groveling. "I never doubted you. You're pretty. You're …"

"Bradford," Amanda said, cutting him off, "remember how you said you never lose?"

"I certainly do," he replied. "And with your victory tonight, my perfect record continues."

Amanda shook her head. "Guess again, locust lips. You just lost me."

I had to turn away so Bradford wouldn't see me smiling. "Way to go, Amanda," I mumbled under my breath. My admiration for my sister had just gone through the roof.

Finding my way to Sam and Felix, I pulled them aside. "Okay, we made it through tonight. Now if everything comes together tomorrow, we'll have it made."

17

Sweeter than Honey

The Bug-Off Banquet took place on the last day of the Locust Festival. People gathered from all around for food and socializing. Most of all, they wanted to see who would win the Bug-Off and the $5,000 first prize.

Considering that I didn't even have a locust entered, I felt pretty good. It's amazing how much better life is when kindness motivates you instead of greed and selfishness. I guess if Jesus loved me enough to give His life for me, I could give up a small fortune for my sister. No, I wouldn't be the next Locust Legend, but I had a bigger heart, and that was worth far more than $5,000.

As soon as I arrived at the picnic grounds, I found who I was looking for. The Munsters, I mean Spiffs, were sitting at a table, enjoying the banquet. Sam already had apologized, but now it was my turn. "I'm sorry we robbed your garden," I said. "I'm the one who talked Sam and Felix into it."

They were quick to forgive me and only asked that next time I wait for permission. Leaving the Spiffs, I met up with Sam and Felix. Sam had the present wrapped in beautiful flowered wrapping paper.

"Well?" Sam asked, handing me the box. "What do you think?"

"It looks great," I said. "Are you sure she's here?"

Sam shrugged. "She's supposed to be."

We looked over the crowd sitting at picnic tables, keeping an eye on the stage. Soon the Bug-Off winner would be announced.

"There she is," Felix said. Sam and I looked in the direction Felix was pointing. Aunt Kathy sat at a table by herself, off to the side of the stage. Without being seen, we worked our way through the chairs and tables.

"Happy B-day!" we exclaimed. I placed the gift on the table in front of Aunt Kathy.

She looked up at us and smiled, totally shocked. "But it's not my birthday."

"We meant *Bee-day*," Sam said with a laugh. "Go ahead and open it." We grinned from ear to ear as Aunt Kathy peeled back the paper and opened the box.

"How did you find this?" she asked, stunned. Neatly folded in the box was the sting-proof suit. She lifted it out and hugged it like an old friend.

"We bought it back," Sam explained. "We know how much the bee farm means to you. We don't want you to give up."

"Yeah," I added. "We'll even work for free. And this time we'll bring Felix." I introduced him to Aunt Kathy. "Felix is an insect expert."

"I wouldn't go that far," Felix said. "But I've definitely learned a few things about bugs in the last week."

Aunt Kathy shook Felix's hand. "From what I have heard, you developed quite the locust attractor."

"Actually, we all developed it," Felix explained. "But it still didn't win Willie the contest."

"Well, if you can modify it to attract bees, I'd be grateful. In fact, so would a lot of other bee farmers."

"Sounds like a money-maker to me," Felix said.

"All I want to do is earn enough to fix Orville's truck," I said. "Other than that, I'm happy."

"Willie, I'm so sorry I haven't paid you for the work you did," Aunt Kathy apologized. "Right now it's all I can do to put food on the table and pay the bills, at least most of them." She looked down, her face filled with sorrow. The joy of the moment had passed too soon.

"Good afternoon, locust lovers," the master of ceremonies announced, standing at the podium. Everyone in the audience stared at the stage, including Marvin Bink, who sat at the very front table, beaming from ear to ear.

"Join me in celebrating this year's Bug-Off winning locust," the emcee said. A large aquarium was carried on stage with the winning locust displayed inside. A video camera projected the locust onto a big screen. Everyone applauded the giant bug.

"The question remains," the master of ceremonies continued, "who entered the winning locust?" A hush swept over the crowd as we waited with anticipation.

The master of ceremonies cleared his throat. "Ladies and gentlemen, the moment you have all been waiting for. This year's Bug-Off champion is ... drumroll, please ... Katherine Stewart."

"Aunt Kathy?" we said together, totally shocked.

Standing up, Aunt Kathy looked as surprised as we were. "When the locusts scared off my bees, I caught the biggest one. But I had no idea it would win," she said.

An usher came forward to lead Aunt Kathy to the stage. The mayor joined her there and handed her an oversize check for $5,000.

"How does that make you feel?" the mayor asked.

"Sweeter than honey!" Aunt Kathy said, lifting the check over her head. Tears rolled down her checks as the photographers gathered around. I just shook my head in awe, amazed at how God had worked everything out so well, in ways I never would have expected.

Grumbling under his breath, Marvin Bink stomped by without even looking at me. Then I remembered Aunt Kathy's favorite verse. "Unless the Lord builds the house, its builders labor in vain." Sure, hard work is important, but trusting the Lord is more important by far.

"It's payday," Aunt Kathy said as soon as she returned to the table. "And not just for the days you worked, but for the days yet to come."

She meant what she said. As soon as she cashed the check, I had enough money to fix Orville's truck. And as for modifying the locust concentrate to attract bees, it worked even better than expected. How much better?

Well, let's just say they don't call me Wave Ruler Willie for nothing.

① iNVASiON from planet X

Willie Plummet

② submarine SaNDWiCHeD

the misadventures of Willie Plummet

③ you can do I can do Better

the misadventures Willie Plummet

④ ballistic BUGS

the misadventures of Willie Plummet

battle of the BANDS

the misadventures of Willie Plummet

⑤ Gold Flakes for Breakfast

the misadventures of Willie Plummet

Look for all these **exciting** WiLLiE PLUMMET misadventures at your local Christian **bookstore!**